MORENO VALLEY PUBLIC LIBRARY
D0345194

the TOMB

S. A. BODEEN

Feiwel and Friends
New York

A Feiwel and Friends Book
An imprint of Macmillan Publishing Group, LLC
175 Fifth Avenue, New York, NY 10010

Printed in the United States of America
by LSC Communications, Harrisonburg, Virginia.

Library of Congress Cataloging-in-Publication Data is available.

ISBN 978-1-250-05555-2 (hardcover) / ISBN 978-1-250-29651-1 (ebook)

Book design by Erin Schell

Feiwel and Friends logo designed by Filomena Tuosto

First Edition, 2018

For Scott Mendel,
the one person in my life
who only calls with good news

1

Kiva sensed Seth before she saw him.

Uncomfortable on the rough sycamore bench, she bent low over a lengthy scroll. The fingers of her left hand gripped the stylus and she bit her lower lip, concentrating so hard, as usual, that she didn't even notice one strap of her pale yellow kalasiri slip off her shoulder.

Suddenly, the equation in her head vanished.

The air flowing in the room seemed to cease.

Startled, she swept her gaze down the long table.

The others in her class were still absorbed in their own studies. Ada's nose nearly touched the table as she pressed figures onto the papyrus, her eyes hidden behind a curtain of dark, glossy hair. The twins Rom and Rem murmured over the work in front of them, heads so close together that it was hard to tell where one's curly black hair ended and the other's began.

There was no reason for Kiva to be aware of the prince of Alexandria.

She turned.

Her eyes confirmed what her gut already knew.

Seth was a bit taller than when she last caught a glimpse of him, six months ago at the festival of the moon. His chest, bare beneath the gold ram's head amulet strung on a chunky strand of lapis, was more filled out; his arms, the right bicep wrapped several times by a silver, red-jewel-eyed viper, more muscular. A strip of leopard fur lined the waist of his blue knee-length shendyt, and his dark head was completely shaved in the style of his father, the Pharaoh, which made him seem older than fifteen.

But those brown eyes, their size accented by the thick rim of jet-black kohl, had not changed from when he was a child, playing hide-and-seek with her in clumps of bulrushes at the river's edge. His chin dipped ever so slightly. "Kiva."

Out of habit, Kiva's fingers drifted to the red woven bracelet on her arm, tracing the soft, worn ridges she knew so well. "Seth." After so long, his name sounded strange when she said it aloud.

The stylus fell out of Ada's hand and her eyes widened.

The twins straightened up when they noticed the prince, then turned their attention to Kiva.

Annoyed at Seth for catching her off guard, especially in front of the others, part of her wanted to turn back around, start writing again, pretend she hadn't seen him.

Or, perhaps, pretend that she didn't care.

Neither seemed like an option at the moment, particularly since her peers seemed to be breathlessly awaiting her reaction to his presence.

Gods. She stood, smoothed the sheath that fell to her ankles, and held her head high. A few quick strides erased the space between them.

He stepped back a foot, as if not wanting to stand too close.

Kiva was near enough to tell she'd been off; the prince had grown more than an inch or two. Her voice projected far greater confidence than she felt. "This is a surprise."

Seth didn't answer. His gaze drifted slowly around the room, paused on the others.

Ada blushed and buried her head in her scroll.

Rom raised a hand halfway in a wave, stopped short by Rem's elbow to his ribs.

A corner of Seth's mouth turned up, as if amused.

"What?" Kiva asked. "Is something funny?"

He gazed down and bent forward, as if to share a secret. She held her breath.

Every part of her tried hard not to care, but failed. She still held out hope that he would offer words, a medicine to heal the hurt, answers to her questions of the past three years.

She longed for him to call her by the nickname only he used. That would be all it took for her to know he still cared.

Please say it, please please . . .

His voice was deeper than she remembered, but quiet. "Your world—"

Two giggling girls from the class below them entered the room, interrupting. They stopped when they saw the prince and stood there openmouthed.

Kiva grabbed Seth's arm and pulled him out to the courtyard bathed bright by the midday Egyptian sun.

The prince stared at her hand with disdain.

"Sorry." She let go. "Please. Finish."

"Prince! There you are." A woman rushed across the manicured plaza, her ebony, chin-length hair bouncing, a red cape draped over her white kalasiri—official uniform of the palace's royal vizier—that flowed out behind her.

Kiva frowned. "What is my mother doing here?"

"Sabra's here for me. Thought I lost her, but she's faster than I expected." He winked. Then, he casually slid her strap back up on her shoulder.

In that moment he became the prince Kiva used to know, her best friend from the time she was four.

Her heartbeat sped up.

Had he slipped away from the palace to give her a message? Why seek her out after avoiding her for so long? Her long-slumbering hopes roused, dampening the slightest bit as her mother continued to bear down on them.

"Finish what you were saying," Kiva spoke fast. "My world what?"

"Prince!" Her harried mother was almost upon them. "We need to return to the palace."

"Your world"—Seth pointed at Kiva, then gestured at the door, as if to include the others—"is as you see it to be." He bent down, his head close to hers, then whispered, "Until it isn't."

She wanted to ask what he meant, but her mother reached them before she had a chance.

Seth said, "I must return to the palace."

"What?" Kiva stared up at him. That was it? He was leaving?

Kiva didn't want him to go. She wanted more than anything to believe that he had come to see her, that he *wanted* to see her. "You could stay." She pointed inside. "Our class would be happy to see you."

Seth's laugh was not kind. Once again, he was a stranger. "That's not a good idea." The prince turned his back and strolled across the courtyard.

Kiva's stomach clenched.

Had he come only to bother her?

Hot tears threatened.

Sabra took her daughter's hand. "What did he say to you?"

Kiva stared at Seth's back. "Nothing." The lump in her throat made the word hitch as it came out. "He said nothing."

Sabra pressed her lips to Kiva's forehead. "I'll see you at home." She followed the prince around the row of low sun-dried brick buildings.

Kiva stared at the green hill that bordered one edge of the school grounds. It seemed like yesterday that she and Seth rolled down the mild grade, laughing when they ended up a tangled heap at the bottom.

The lovely setting grew blurry through her tears.

No. Not yesterday.

"Another lifetime." She wiped her face and avoided looking at the others when she went back inside and rolled up her scroll.

Ada asked, "What did he want?"

Rom said, "No one cares what the stupid prince wanted."

"He used to be our friend," said Rem.

Rom said, "And now he's too good for us."

"He didn't ever *have* to be our friend," said Ada.

Kiva felt anger swell. "He was always *my* friend."

"Until he wasn't." But Rem's words were not unkind, simply honest. "Better to forget that we ever knew him as anything other than the prince."

Kiva slammed her scroll on a side table and headed out the doorway.

"It isn't time to leave yet," called Ada.

Kiva ignored her.

Outside, past the buildings, the river sparkled in the hot sun. She removed her sandals and let them dangle by their straps from a fingertip. Her bare feet scuffed the rough path, dust puffing up with each step.

She knelt on the grassy riverbank and leaned over, staring into the water. Inside the blunt frame of her dark hair, her face was a vague oval. She touched the surface, then brought her wet, cool hand up to her cheek.

Quiet moments gave her too much time to think.

Not a welcome thing.

How could she believe, even for a second, that Seth actually cared enough to want to see her?

It was time to stop thinking of him as her best friend.

He was nothing but a former friend.

The sooner she dealt with it, the better.

Kiva tossed a stick in the water. Her reflection broke into ripples.

If only it were as easy to break her train of thought. She desperately needed something else in her head besides the prince.

She got to her feet and leaned down to wipe a bit of dust off the bottom of her dress. An overturned beetle caught her eye. With flailing appendages, the insect struggled to right itself. "Someone else is having a bad day." Gently, Kiva tipped the bug over and watched it skitter away before she headed toward home.

First, she stopped at a small dwelling, identical to the one next door that she shared with her mother. She wiped her sweaty face on her sleeve and stepped back into the sandals before pausing inside the doorway. "Fai?" She moved farther into the dim, cool interior. "Are you here?"

Fai, Alexandria's physician, was also Kiva's willing mentor. The elder woman's voice came from another room. "You're early."

Kiva considered a lie, perhaps that school was let out early. But Fai had a sixth sense about such things, leaving truth as the better choice. "I had enough for the day."

Fai appeared in a looser fitting sheath than the girl's, silver hair nearly glowing, smile raising deep lines in her dark, weathered face. As always, she neither judged nor scolded. "Some days are like that. I'm glad you're here." She held out a laundered but bloodstained apron. "You'll need this."

Kiva followed Fai into her laboratory.

Flaming torches lit the windowless, low-ceilinged room. The walls were lined with shelves on which rows of preserved, coiled cobras floated in large glass jars full of clear liquid, a sight that always sent a shiver down Kiva's spine. She squinted at the pink belly of a tiny dead pig on the rough wooden table in the center of the room.

"Stillborn this morning," said Fai.

Kiva poked a finger into the pig's stiff, cold hide.

"You need to focus," said Fai.

"I will." But as soon as she tried to make her mind blank, Seth's words echoed. *Your world is as you see it to be. Until it isn't.*

For nearly three years her former best friend doesn't speak to her, and when he does lower himself enough to actually acknowledge her existence? He offers nothing but nonsense. And laughs at her when she asks him to come inside the place where they used to spend hours together.

Why wouldn't he want to take a few moments to speak with the others?

With her?

"You need to put aside your troubles, Kiva." Fai cleared her throat. "One day your patient will be alive. Probably human." The wrinkles in the older woman's forehead deepened. "And I suspect they won't appreciate crooked stitches. Or a thick scar."

"I know." Kiva tied the apron at the back of her neck, then picked up the blade in her left hand and steadied it.

The Pharaoh's son wasn't worth another thought. Yes, it was maddening that one sentence from Seth could affect her this way, especially since she thought she'd gotten past the way he'd changed. Despite the different status of their families in the community, their class of five had been friends from the time they started school.

But Seth's mother died of an illness when they were twelve.

Soon after, he stopped coming to school and became a recluse in the palace.

Kiva understood that Seth had been grieving. She wanted to be there for him and waited patiently for him to reach out to her. But he never did. As the years passed, her sympathy waned. She couldn't help feeling he had abandoned them.

No.

Kiva bit her bottom lip.

He'd abandoned *her*.

"Start here." Fai set a finger along the pig's throat and drew it straight down to the belly. "You'll be able to practice many stitches."

Kiva set the blade on flesh and pushed, drawing it down the corpse, opening up a neat, expert incision.

Fai clicked her tongue. "Your hands have grown so steady."

Kiva reached the end and lifted the blade, then wiped it on her apron. She tried to focus on the task, the thing she loved most. Medicine.

Still, Seth's face, now almost a stranger's, lingered in her head. Three years had passed since his mother died and he no longer spoke to anyone his own age.

The others appeared not to mind as much, if at all.

Rom and Rem had each other. Ada had her younger sister.

Kiva had Seth.

Until she didn't.

His sudden appearance at school, a reminder of what she had lost, only made things worse.

His words, his cruel laugh, his sudden exit made Kiva feel deflated. She longed for a connection with him, a sign that he was back after the last three years.

Instead, he muttered pointless, condescending words that did nothing but make her scold herself for wasting time on the absurd belief that their friendship could be salvaged.

"Kiva?"

"What?" Her gaze lifted.

"I said you can start stitching now." Fai pointed at the open belly. "Remember, tight and even. And keep in mind your future patient may be awake for the process. Do your best not to tug."

Kiva nodded.

"I'll go make some tea."

Kiva threaded the needle with sinew, then poked it through one edge of the skin, pulling it tight on the other side. She did another stitch and another, methodically sealing the pig's belly back together.

If only all things in her life were as easy to mend.

Suddenly, the floor shook.

She dropped the needle and grabbed the edge of the table to keep from falling, breaking the longish nail on one index finger in the process. "Fai!" A glass jar fell off a shelf and exploded at her feet. Slimy liquid drenched her legs as the freed cobra uncoiled and, as if still alive, slid toward her.

Kiva shrieked and jumped away.

Part of the ceiling fell and clipped her shoulder. She dove under the table, edging farther away from the expanding snake.

Fai ran into the room and crawled under to join her.

Debris continued to crash around them as they huddled together. Kiva rubbed her shoulder as her heart seemed determined to pound a path out of her chest. "What's happening?"

Fai gripped Kiva's trembling hand. "An earthquake. It has to be an earthquake." But there was little conviction in her words, and her hand was as unsteady as the girl's. "We need to get in the open." She pulled Kiva toward the door.

Outside the ground still trembled, but there was less danger with nothing to fall on them.

Kiva stared up. The sky remained cloudless and blue, the sun still shone.

But screams seemed to come from everywhere.

Kiva touched her shoulder and winced. "I think that I hurt—"

"You'll live," said Fai.

Kiva didn't have time to consider the physician's lack of empathy, because her grip on Fai's hand tightened. "My mother!"

"The palace is strong." Fai smiled faintly. "No worries there."

Kiva remembered the other member of their household. "Sasha!" Kiva turned to run to her house, but Fai held tight to her hand.

"Wait until it stops."

Tears filled Kiva's eyes.

"Cats can take care of themselves. You'll see."

As if to prove her right, a black cat streaked out of Kiva's house.

"Sasha!"

But the cat kept going, around the corner of Fai's house.

Kiva started to follow, but then the rumbling ceased.

"Sasha will come back," said Fai. "I need to see if anyone is hurt. Run back and get the black bag from my laboratory."

Kiva hurried. But inside Fai's house, she moved slowly as she picked her way through the rubble of furniture and things that had tumbled from shelves. In the lab itself, the ceiling had fallen in, breaking the table. The pig's legs stuck out from a slab of stone and she squatted beside it.

The ceiling could have crushed her just as easily.

A bit of red in the debris caught her eye and she plucked it out. "Oh no." Half of her bracelet, the one she wore day in and day out. The one Seth had made for her twelfth birthday, a few weeks before his mother died.

When the chunk of ceiling had hit her, the bracelet must have been torn apart. In the chaos, she hadn't even noticed.

She sighed and dropped the ruined bracelet onto the dead pig.

Maybe it was a sign.

And, thanks to the prince himself, she suspected it would be quite easy indeed to never cross her former best friend's path again.

2

Fai sent Kiva home, where Sasha waited at the front door, a dead mouse at her front paws.

Kiva made a face. "Nice." She scooped up the cat and went inside, fingers crossed the place wouldn't be in ruins. A clay plate lay shattered on the floor, and one of the chairs by the table tilted, as if lame in one leg. But other than a few things askew on shelves, the place was not nearly as damaged as Fai's laboratory.

Kiva cleaned up the plate and straightened the things on the shelves. She righted a vase with blooming white narcissus flowers she'd picked that morning and set it back on the table. Her stomach growled and she grabbed a handful of dates. She knew it was selfish to hope that her mother would go to the market and bring home a chunk of fish. Sabra was late and probably had far too much to manage in the palace to worry about Kiva's favorite meal. Childish, she supposed, to be searching for comfort after the day she'd had.

The cat jumped onto the large blue-striped cushion near the window. Kiva plopped down, snuggling Sasha in her lap as she stroked her sleek fur. Seth had always loved the cat.

Kiva groaned.

Again, the moment her mind had time to wander, who did she think about?

But it was hard not to think about Seth after seeing him. At one time, he'd spent more hours in Kiva's home than his own. He told her the palace was too big and he liked the smaller houses better. His mother, Nell, had been close to Sabra. Best friends, in fact, and the children often had sleepovers. Never at the palace, which was fine with Seth.

Kiva didn't mind. She only wanted to be with her best friend, she didn't care where.

Then, about four months before Kiva turned twelve, Nell became ill. Kiva's twelfth birthday was the last time she saw her. Kiva insisted on wearing her new blue sheath that day, even though it was slightly too big and the straps kept slipping from her shoulders. She also convinced her mother to line her eyes with kohl and rub ochre on her lips.

Sabra had invited Fai as well. That day, Nell looked

beautiful and healthy. But the adults spoke unfamiliar words in hushed tones when they thought the children weren't listening.

Kiva asked Seth, "Is something wrong with your mother?"

His hair was shaved but for a side-lock, which he tugged. "She's sick."

"But she looks fine."

Worry showed in his face. "She stays in her room a lot. I only see her a little each morning."

Kiva touched his arm. "Maybe she'll feel better soon."

"Maybe." He reached into the waist of his shendyt and held out a small package wrapped in a slightly crooked palm-frond bow. "Happy birthday, Keeves."

"But your parents already gave me—"

"I know," he interrupted. "This is from me."

Kiva undid the stiff makeshift ribbon. The palm fronds fell apart, revealing a bracelet woven from bright red linen, a delicate trail of white chevrons lining the edges. She smiled. "It's beautiful."

Seth shook his head. "It's just a small thing. I made it, but the pattern got a little crooked on that end and—"

Kiva squeezed his hand. "It's perfect. I love it." She held it out. "Put it on me?"

Seth concentrated so hard on tying the bracelet that he stuck his tongue out.

Kiva grinned.

He frowned. "Too tight?"

"No." She circled her wrist in the air. "Just right. Thank you." She leaned forward and pecked him on the cheek. Her lips left a red smear, which she tried to wipe off with a finger. "Sorry."

"You're pretty without it." Seth's gaze dropped to her arm, where one of her straps had fallen. He slid it back up, and his finger lingered on her shoulder.

"Kids," Sabra called. "Time to eat."

Less than a month later, Nell was gone.

The school closed down for a week, and Seth was absent after it reopened, which seemed only natural. He'd lost his mother.

But he didn't return.

The others grew used to his empty seat next to Kiva's at the long classroom table.

Kiva could not.

Seth's scroll remained there, next to hers. One day she came to school and it was gone. "Where is it?" she cried.

"We moved it out of the way." Ada pointed to the side table.

"Don't ever touch it!" Kiva moved the scroll back to Seth's place.

When they came back after summer break that year, the scroll was gone.

She didn't ask where it went.

Because that might make it seem like she cared. And she didn't want anyone to know that she still did, because by then, she hadn't seen or spoken to her best friend for over a year.

Only a fool would keep hoping after that much time had passed.

Occasionally she saw Seth at community celebrations and state dinners that she was forced to attend with her mother. The first time, she had been excited, waving at him to try to get his attention.

But he didn't wave back, even though she was certain he noticed her.

The next time, she didn't bother to wave. Fortunately, there were often many people, and it was easy to sit at opposite ends of the massive table.

In all that time, they hadn't come face-to-face.

Until today. The day the earth shook for the first time Kiva could ever remember. "It's a sign, Sasha." Kiva tapped the cat's warm pink nose. "A big sign."

She kept busy as she waited for her mother to come home. Finally, near sunset, the door creaked open.

"Kiva?"

Kiva pushed the cat off her lap and stood. "Mom?"

"Oh, I was so worried." Sabra embraced Kiva, holding her far longer than usual. "Are you all right?"

Kiva nodded. "I was with Fai. We hid under the table."

"I'm so sorry I wasn't here. The palace was a mess and—" Her mother sounded odd. The day had been a strain for everyone, but there was something else. Sabra sat on the cushion and stroked the cat.

Kiva's shoulders tensed.

Her mother was not a fan of Sasha. In fact, she never touched the cat except to boot her outside when she bestowed one of her rodent gifts upon them.

So she asked, "What's wrong?"

"I have news." Sabra patted the cushion next to her.

Kiva sat down, not taking her gaze away from her mother's. "It's bad?"

"Well, it's . . ." Sabra let out a long breath. "Yes. The worst."

Her mother seemed more anxious than stricken. Sabra put an arm around Kiva's shoulders. "I need you to be brave."

Kiva's hands balled into fists. "Tell me."

"The earthquake caused . . . damage at the palace."

"Was anyone hurt?" She didn't understand why her mother wasn't just telling her.

Sabra nodded.

"Bad?"

Sabra took a deep breath and blew it out. "Seth was killed."

Kiva drew back. "What?"

"I'm so sorry." Sabra set a hand on Kiva's face. "I know how close you were and—"

"No." Kiva shook off her mother's arm and stood up.

"I know it's hard to hear, but he didn't suffer and—"

"No!" Kiva's face grew hot and her hands clenched once more. "I mean we're not close anymore, we're not even friends, and I never wanted to see him again anyway. This makes it that much easier!" Kiva took a big gulp of air that turned into a sob on its way back out.

Sabra swept her into her arms.

Tears filled Kiva's eyes. An invisible hand clutched her insides, making it impossible to breathe.

Why did it have to happen today?

She had just seen Seth again, after so long. She was so close to being able to not care about him anymore. And now . . . she couldn't help it.

Finally, between sobs, she said, "I missed him . . . so much . . ." She shuddered. "Today . . . I thought . . . he came back . . . to be my friend." She broke down again, unable to finish.

But he didn't want to be her friend. And even if he did change his mind, it doesn't matter. He's gone forever.

Sabra stroked Kiva's hair. "It'll be all right."

"No it won't," she muttered into her mother's shoulder.

"Just give it time and you'll see. It's not as bad as you think."

"How can you say that?" Kiva wiped her face on her sleeve and sat up, staring at her mother. "He's dead."

Sabra looked down.

Kiva didn't understand. She didn't want to. "I'm going for a walk."

"You should eat, sweetheart."

"I want to be alone."

Outside, Kiva sprinted along the riverbank, parallel to the crimson setting sun. A group of voices rose, panicked by the aftermath of the shaking. She paused at the shadowed edge of a dwelling and crept forward, panting, hands on the rough bricks.

She listened.

"There's destruction all over."

"There's never been a quake before."

"Was anyone hurt?"

She waited for someone to mention the prince's death.

No one seemed to be aware of it yet.

She wished she wasn't.

Kiva ran farther along the river, stopping at a bend beyond the cluster of houses. There, she knelt beside a clump of reeds, out of sight from anyone coming from that direction, and caught her breath.

She didn't think she could miss Seth any more than she already did, but this was worse. This was so final.

At least, for the past three years, there had been some optimism.

Even after today, with her anger and subsequent decision not to care, there always had to be a tiny sliver of faith that he would come to his senses.

But now?

All hope died along with the prince.

Kiva's throat grew thick, her eyes warm, and she began to cry again.

She couldn't believe he was gone. Had he thought of her before the end? Maybe he even wished he had said more to her that afternoon. Been nicer.

Been her friend again.

"No." She didn't like picturing his last moments being filled with regrets.

Even though she'd been mad at Seth for a long time, and he hadn't been the best friend to her, she wanted his last moments to be full of peace and good memories of his life.

At least he didn't have to miss his mother anymore.

She sniffled.

Where was Seth at that very moment?

Probably in a quiet, candlelit room in the palace.

The palace priest, Natron, would have been called in as the chief embalmer. She pictured him wearing the jackal head of the god Anubis as he regarded the prince's body.

She wiped her eyes on her sleeve.

The process was nothing new to her; she'd been pretending to make mummies since she was a child, Seth often her willing play victim.

The memory brought a wan smile to her face.

First, there would be an epic battle in which the prince would meet a fitting heroic and dramatic end. Kiva would then arrange his body as she assumed the role of priest and chief embalmer.

But somewhere, that very moment, Seth was not pretending.

This time, his end was real.

Still, it hurt less to focus on the anatomical aspect: the concrete skin and bones that remained, rather than the weightless, abstract mind and soul that did not.

Natron would insert a hook through a hole near the nose and pull out part of the brain. Then he would use a flint knife to cut on the left side of the body near the stomach, and all the contents of the abdomen would be removed. The priest would then wash the cavity a first time using palm wine, a second with various spices. Then the body, Seth's body, would be filled with pure myrrh, cassia, and other aromatics.

The lungs, intestines, stomach, and liver would be sealed in canopic jars carved from limestone. But the heart . . .

Seth's heart would be placed back inside his body.

Perhaps, at that very moment, Natron held the prince's heart in his hands.

Kiva's face crumpled and more tears leaked out.

Thinking about Seth's heart hurt her own far too much.

"Be a doctor." Kiva spoke the words aloud and rocked back and forth as she rubbed the rough edge of her broken nail. "Focus. What comes next?"

After rinsing the insides of Seth's body with wine and spices—the most precious, befitting his royal stature—Natron would cover the corpse for at least forty days. After about seventy, the body would be wrapped in linen strips and placed in a wooden sarcophagus inside the burial chamber.

The tomb.

Some of them were huge.

The Seth she knew, her best friend, wouldn't have liked that. If he found the palace to be echoing and lonely, imagine how he would find a massive tomb for all eternity.

But he wouldn't even know he was in a tomb, he wouldn't have a chance to be lonely.

The loneliness would dwell with her, because she was the one left behind.

Kiva hugged her knees to her chest.

In the time she'd been sitting at the shore, night had fallen. Lights twinkled from the small homes along the river. She couldn't stay there forever.

When Kiva returned home she crept in the window and lay down on her bed. She would go back out later and enter through the front. Sabra meant well, but Kiva didn't feel like talking.

Voices came from the front of the house.

Her mother.

And who else?

She didn't care to listen.

Until her mother's voice rose. "Who decided this?"

Kiva opened the door a crack.

Fai was speaking. "We didn't expect it to happen this way. But our hands are forced."

What were they talking about?

"Fai, I don't understand why this is the only way. Seth is already gone."

Fai cleared her throat. "He can't go alone. You of all people should know that."

"Fai, you know it could easily be one of us, one of the adults. Is this the right thing to do?"

"This is the only way. It will satisfy—"

"Who?" demanded Sabra. "Who will it satisfy?"

"You know who! The ones that will cause trouble if Seth is not accompanied. The dissenters demanded this."

Kiva frowned.

Seth was dead. Why did anyone need to be sent with him?

Kiva sucked in a breath. Did they mean a retainer sacrifice?

Some believed that royals must be accompanied into the afterlife by servants to care for them. Kiva heard stories about the practice, but no royal had ever been entombed in her lifetime. Seth's mother's mummy was in a family crypt, awaiting the Pharaoh's death.

Kiva had never seen a sacrifice, and until now she didn't believe it to be something that actually occurred.

"But a child?" Kiva's mother was talking once again. "Why must it be a child?"

Kiva exhaled. If the retainer sacrifice was going to be a child, then it had to be someone she knew.

She braced herself as she ran through the list of people she cared for. Ada, Rem, Rom: she'd feel terrible if it was any of them. Anyone else, of course she'd feel bad for them and their family.

The whole idea was too awful to even consider.

Sabra asked Fai, "Tell me the truth. Are you part of it?"

"I argued with them for hours. You know that!"

"It could be anyone else." Sabra sniffled.

Was her mother crying? She didn't know when she'd last seen her mother cry. The day had been hard on everyone, and maybe her more than most.

"Sabra." Fai's tone was quiet, comforting. "I care for her as much as you do."

Kiva froze.

"But in the end, she's my child." Sabra sobbed. "Kiva is mine."

Oh Gods, thought Kiva. *It's me.*

She closed the door and leaned back against it.

The sacrifice is me. Her legs gave out and she slid to the floor.

"No. I won't do it," she whispered.

But why was she chosen?

Was it because she and Seth had been close? Had the Pharaoh made the final decision in his shock and grief? She was Sabra's daughter—surely it meant something to spare the child of someone so important to the royal family.

Kiva longed to burst into her mother and Fai's conversation and beg them to find another solution. But she couldn't let them know she'd heard.

Quickly, she rose and slipped out the window. She thought about drying her tears, but realized they would attribute her sadness to Seth.

She walked to the front and pushed the door open.

The two women froze when they saw her. Sabra's face was tear-stained, her eyes red.

Kiva shut the door behind her. "Sorry I was so long."

Her mother forced a small smile. "Are you hungry?"

Kiva caught her breath. Her mother had just been discussing her death, and she wanted Kiva to eat?

Food was not a priority for Kiva. "I'm tired. I'm going to bed."

Sabra stood and gave her a long hug. Too long for a simple goodnight.

That hug was definitely of the sorry-you-are-going-to-be-sacrificed nature.

Fai called, "Good night, dear."

But Kiva couldn't even look at her.

In her room, she shut the door and fell into bed.

She was heartbroken over Seth, and sorry that he was gone. But she did not intend to go with him.

Kiva needed a plan.

Fortunately, the traditions and protocols of entombment would give her roughly seventy days to make one.

Kiva woke and jerked upright. Sasha lay curled at her feet.

Events of the previous day rushed back.

Seth at school.

The earthquake.

Seth *dead.*

And she was to accompany him.

As a sacrifice.

But she had to act normal, not let on that she knew. There was plenty of time to come up with an escape plan.

Kiva slipped out of bed and padded into the main room.

Sabra sat at the table, sipping tea. Her eyes were red. "Good morning."

Kiva sat down across from her, hands clasped together on the table. "You're not at the palace."

"No work today."

"Because of the earthquake yesterday?"

"No. Sweetheart . . ." Sabra set a hand on Kiva's. "The earthquake was the day the prince died."

Kiva frowned. "Which was *yesterday*."

"It was over two months ago."

"That's impossible." Kiva stared at the vase of narcissus flowers that she had picked the morning before. But they were wilted to ugliness. She touched one and it turned to dust. *Wasn't it?*

Sabra shifted in her chair. "Kiva, you're confused. Maybe you're upset because today is Seth's funeral."

Kiva yanked her hand back. "What?"

"Losing Seth was traumatic. But you've been dealing with it all so . . . admirably." Sabra smiled a little. "I'm so proud."

Kiva's mind raced.

Was her mother delusional?

There was no way so much time could have passed.

Out of habit, her fingers went to her wrist. Failing to find the bracelet, she rubbed the rough edge of her broken nail.

She froze as she gaped at her index finger.

The nail was still as short as when she broke it in Fai's lab the day of the earthquake.

Yesterday.

Her mother was lying.

"Kiva, I know this has been a terrible time for you. And I hope all the rest has helped you deal with Seth's death."

"Rest?"

"Fai insisted the sleeping medicine would help—"

"Sleeping medicine?"

Her mother nodded. "You were so upset, it was the only thing that got you to sleep. I know you've slept far too much these past weeks, but—"

Kiva needed to get away from the lies. "I have things to do before the funeral."

"I thought we could spend time together, talk about—"

"Talk about what?" snapped Kiva. "I heard you and Fai." She held a hand flat on her chest. "Maybe we should talk about me being dead in a few hours!"

"But you won't be—" Sabra stopped.

"Are you saying I'm not going to be the sacrifice?"

"True, it is you; you've known for weeks."

"No I haven't. You're lying." Kiva rubbed the edge of her fingernail to remind herself that she wasn't imagining things. The flowers were dead, but there was no explaining that broken nail.

Her mother swallowed. "I want to make more memories today, while we have a chance."

"Haven't we had *over two months* to do that?"

Sabra's eyes widened. "Yes." She stared at the table. "You're right."

"I'll be in my room." There, Kiva quickly dressed and put on sandals. She didn't know what was going on, but she did know that her mother couldn't be trusted.

She went over to the window. There was no way she was going to let them take her.

When she was younger, she often snuck out to meet Seth after bedtime. They often did nothing but sit beside each other on the moonlit riverbank, throw sticks into the water, and watch them spin in the current.

A lump grew in her throat and tears welled up.

Her grief for him was so fresh.

"There's no way I could have been feeling this way for over two months." Kiva hoisted herself up onto the sill and dropped to the dirt outside. She jogged along the path with no extra clothes or supplies, no clear plan as to a destination.

What she needed most was to find someone who would tell her the truth.

Ada's house was nearby.

Her friend sat under a date palm, crying into her hands.

"Ada? Why are you crying?"

Ada looked up, her eyes swollen, face blotchy. "Why aren't *you*?"

Kiva plopped down on the ground beside her. "Will you tell me what's going on?"

"What are you talking about?' Ada wiped her eyes on her hand. "Today is Seth's funeral."

"I know. But . . . doesn't it feel too soon?"

"It's been over two months."

Kiva sighed.

That again. Why was she the only one who didn't think so much time had passed? "Right." Maybe she should test Ava. "But . . . what have we been doing for the last two months?"

"Doing?" Ada frowned. "We've been going to school. You've been helping me with Maxwell's equations."

"What? You have no idea how to do that."

"Yesterday you told me I was getting it! I think it was yesterday. Now you're just confusing me, Kiva." Ada scowled. "I'm already upset and sad enough."

"*You're* upset?" Kiva was about to lay into her about how being the retainer sacrifice gave her the upper hand on emotion for the day, then wondered why Ada hadn't mentioned it. She scratched her arm. "So, have you heard anything about a retainer sacrifice?"

"A what?"

"Never mind." Kiva stood up. "I have to go."

"See you at the funeral?"

Kiva needed to think.

Ada was as foggy about the supposed passage of time as she was. And why hadn't she heard of Kiva's fate?

"Ada, where's the funeral going to be?"

"Where else would it be?"

"Oh, right." Kiva prodded. "It'll be at the . . ."

"*Tomb.* What's wrong with you?" asked Ada. "It's at the school."

At the school? Why not the palace?

Kiva hurried down the path and around the row of sun-dried brick buildings. She took three steps onto the school's courtyard and froze.

Yesterday, at least what she thought was yesterday, there had been an empty hill.

But there, in front of her, lay a series of limestone brick mastabas built up on three graduated platforms, several dozen steep steps leading up to the wide, dim opening.

The tomb. How did that happen in one day?

Kiva trembled.

She didn't believe any of this.

If the funeral was to take place within hours, where was everyone? Mourners should have been gathering.

Kiva ran to the steps and took them two at a time.

She paused at the mouth of the tomb, wondering why there were no guards. Then she stepped inside a brick hallway, the floor lit by clay pots of oil, burning wicks floating inside. Heart pounding, she moved toward the flickering brightness ahead.

The passageway ended in a rectangular room, a

sarcophagus displayed in the center on a raised dais, surrounded by more of the oil lamps.

Kiva slowly ascended the three steps and stared at the sculpture of Osiris. The green skin of the human-faced god of death and resurrection nearly glowed in the low light as gold strands entwined in his braided beard glittered. His unseeing eyes appeared to track her, and she shivered as she moved closer to the casket.

Was Seth really inside?

Then Kiva noticed a low table on which lay a linen-wrapped body. Her legs threatened to give out, but she made her way there.

She didn't believe her oldest friend was dead until that moment.

"I'm sorry." Kiva ran a trembling hand down the side of the body, skin crawling at the shriveled hardness. "I'm sorry for making you not want to be my friend anymore.

"Whatever I did wrong"—she lowered her head—"I would take it all back." Her eyes closed.

Maybe, if she never opened them again, this wouldn't be true.

Maybe, if she wished with all her heart, this would all turn out to be a bad dream.

Maybe.

She held her breath. *Please please please.*

She couldn't bring herself to open her eyes.

If this was Seth's end, hers wasn't far off.

What would it be like?

Would they kill her beforehand?

Or simply seal her inside and let her starve or die of thirst or lack of air?

"This is pointless."

Her eyes popped opened. She whirled around.

No one was there.

"Hello?"

There was no reply.

She turned back to Seth.

"The others will be there soon." The voice spoke again. *"If your plan is to keep this going, get her out now."*

"Who said that?" Again, Kiva saw no one.

She set her hand back on Seth. "I wish that we—"

Before her eyes, that hand began to disintegrate.

Mesmerized, she gaped as infinitesimal pieces danced in the torchlight like dust.

Kiva could no longer move.

Her body seemed to be shedding itself one cell at a time. Fingers, hand, half her arm and up . . .

Kiva could no longer breathe.

Her body continued to disappear, one insignificant fragment at a time, a floating mosaic of all her parts.

Was this *her* end?

She was the retainer sacrifice.

Piece by piece, the gods were taking her.

Her eyes no longer focused.

In front of her, Seth's body wavered, as if under water.

Odd, but she felt more peace than panic. Death was far kinder than she expected.

She felt herself falling, falling, but she landed nowhere.

After one, final breath, Kiva of Alexandria simply ceased to be.

4

The lamps were extinguished.

There was no sound.

The tomb was a hush, pressing from all sides, stifling.

Kiva was dead.

This was death.

She shivered.

Along with the chill air, she became aware of a dull hum.

Perhaps that was the sound of eternal silence. What one heard when there was no sound at all. The sound of death itself.

She swallowed. Her throat was dry.

And she was breathing.

This wasn't what she expected from death, not at all. But then, she was certainly no expert.

Cautiously, she curled her fingers.

They were sluggish, yet still obeyed.

She wiggled her toes. Same reaction.

At least she seemed to be in one piece again.

She opened her eyes.

Darkness.

She blinked once, twice.

Utter darkness.

Was she blind?

She had always been afraid of the night. Her heartbeat sped up.

Panic, for certain, was not something a dead person felt.

Did that mean she was . . .

"I'm alive! I'm still alive!" She sat straight up. "I'm—"

Lights, brighter than the sun, popped on overhead.

She was not blind.

And this was no tomb.

She covered her eyes with one arm, her clothing soft and fragrant against her face.

Blinking as her eyes adjusted to the glare, Kiva glanced down.

She was on a bed with a colorful red-and-blue-striped cloth. Two separate pieces of clothing—black, and snug but stretchy—covered both her top and bottom, bands of it tighter at her wrists.

She traced raised letters on one of the cuffs.

SV.

She lifted her arm and pressed her nose into her shoulder and inhaled.

The scent was new and lovely, something she had never smelled before.

Like flowers.

But she knew what flowers smelled like, didn't she?

She slid sideways on the bed and stretched out her stiff legs. For as long as she could recall, she'd only worn sheaths, never anything that allowed her to move so freely.

Or anything so soft.

Funny that clothing in the afterlife was to her liking.

She pushed up and off the bed, landed on her bare feet. The blood rushed to her head, prickles of white in front of her eyes. She shut them and leaned on the edge of the bed, legs wobbling.

Why did it feel as though she hadn't stood, let alone walked, for a long time?

Or was this what death was supposed to feel like?

In an effort to get the circulation going, Kiva held on to the bed and squatted a few times as she took note of her strange surroundings.

The slick, cool floor under her feet matched the shiny

white walls, neither like any of the walls or floors in Alexandria.

Kiva pondered for a moment.

This was not entirely unfamiliar: the artificial lights that lit the space like day, the soft material against her skin, the glistening walls and floors . . .

They had learned this in school.

This was all part of the future.

But the future only existed in the minds of the soothsayers, the future seers . . . the dreamers.

She had never truly believed any of it.

Was she dead?

Was she dreaming? A dream that seemed so real she thought she was awake?

Or was the afterlife meant to be the future?

Whoosh.

Kiva jumped as a rush of fresh air came out of a gray slot above her head. She stood there a moment, breathed in the warmth. The flow blew hair into her face. As she went to push it back, she froze at the light brown curls.

Not black and straight.

She pulled a length of hair out and stared. A burial wig of some kind?

She tugged sharply and winced. Definitely attached.

So, she was to be another person in this death dream? A retainer sacrifice wasn't even allowed to be herself?

A chunk of hair held up to her nose revealed fragrance that, again, was pleasing and made her nearly weak with the sensation.

And then a chirping began, a faint, steady rhythm that came from nowhere and everywhere all at once. After a moment, it stopped, but her attention was drawn to a tall cabinet on the far side of the small room, only about ten steps away. A mirror attached to the side showed her the Kiva of this place.

She stared at the girl.

Brown curly hair fell far past her shoulders, except for a light fringe that brushed her eyebrows, beneath which bright green eyes blinked back at her. A spray of freckles dotted her nose and cheeks.

Something flashed at her neck. She pulled a slippery gold necklace out from under her shirt and studied the tiny pendant, an unfamiliar symbol of three intersecting circles.

Kiva took a deep breath and watched as the girl in the mirror did the same. "I guess you're me."

Behind her in the mirror, a tall panel interrupted the smoothness of the wall. As she turned around and stepped closer to examine it, the panel slid to the side and disappeared.

An open doorway lay before her, exposing more darkness beyond.

Apparently this dream was to not only be one of the future, but also one of her nightmares.

She didn't want to go. But how long could she stay there, in that room by herself, wondering what would happen next?

Kiva held her breath and stepped into the black.

More lights flickered on overhead, as bright as the others.

She sighed in relief, then waved a hand in front of her.

Another set of lights turned on.

She took a step. More light.

Another. Still, the illumination kept pace with her motion.

It was either magic . . . or a dream.

She knew magic wasn't real. Death was real, and apparently it felt like a dream.

Kiva stopped and looked behind her.

A short white corridor, with the same slick walls and floor and ceiling, led back to her room.

One option.

She twisted back around.

A dark corridor.

The other option.

"Dreams aren't real."

Hesitation halted her progress, and the lull in motion made her aware of a pulsing underfoot. She squatted and set a hand flat on the floor.

A rhythmic beat; a distinct cadence that repeated, changed slightly, then began once more. She stood back up, more curious than frightened. If she was already dead, then there was nothing to fear.

With the darkness behind her, Kiva had to trust the lights to guide her way. She took a deep breath and moved forward, the pulsing sensation underfoot becoming more pronounced with each step.

After only a few more paces, the lights revealed an end to the brief corridor: a double panel in the shape of a door, like the one in the room she'd left, only larger. Would it open when she reached it?

And what would she find?

Her hand went to rub her wrist. Her empty wrist.

She had forgotten that her bracelet was gone for good.

She missed it.

Was the afterlife supposed to bring such a feeling of loss? There was so much emptiness, so many things that she missed. Her mother. Her cat.

Seth.

Was he there somewhere? That large door . . . did it contain his final resting place?

Was he also in this dream? Or did he have one of his own, a dream that didn't include her?

Maybe she was supposed to have died, but the sacrifice didn't work and she was going to wander these halls of the future until she starved to death or died of thirst or . . .

An especially heavy pulse from beneath her feet spurred her on.

Kiva forced herself to take a step. As she got closer, the panels parted automatically.

A hammering racket blasted her eardrums, the beat a concussion in her head as raspy male voices mingled, yelling words at a rapid tempo, their cadence contrary, almost fighting the beat.

She pressed her hands to her ears.

It turned out death was loud after all.

But there was no time to focus on the sound because the sight before her . . .

Once again, she was overcome with the feeling that this had to be a dream.

The semicircular room in which she stood embodied everything they'd been taught about the future.

A steady line of lights ran from the perimeter of the straight wall behind her, all the way around the arc, before concluding at the edge of the wall to her right: a glowing border between the bare white walls and low ceiling.

Slick and shiny metal cabinets lined the curve on either side. The one on the left was a long, empty counter, but the one on the right had a silver spigot. Everything appeared to be made of materials not found in nature.

Kiva's attention turned to the very front of the room and

the open space where two large black leather chairs with sturdy armrests bellied up to what appeared to be identical gray tables.

One of the chairs was not empty.

Kiva dropped to a crouch, wanting to stay out of sight until she figured out this dream. At last, she was glad for the noise because it concealed her presence.

The person in the chair was dressed in a shirt and pants identical to hers and had dark hair that fell directly above wide, muscular shoulders. Arms stretched up, overhead, with large hands that appeared strong.

Kiva's legs were still weak and unsteady, and she had to rise before she lost her balance.

But she was too abrupt.

Her vision swam for a moment before clearing.

Her stomach growled.

What a strange dream, that she could be weak from hunger.

Her throat was so dry.

The clamor ceased, the abrupt silence nearly as concussive.

Kiva coughed and quickly covered her mouth.

The person stilled, arms slowly lowered. Shoulders slumped a tad, then one hand gestured to the silver faucet on the right. "Water's in there."

The voice was familiar, but not. So close to someone she

knew, but off in some way. Like they were spoken through a tub of water.

The person in the chair swiveled around to face her.

Kiva's legs gave out and she dropped to her knees.

This person . . . was an impossibility.

Except that in a dream, anything was possible.

Because, to Kiva, there could be no other explanation for how she found herself staring into the eyes of the dead prince of Alexandria.

5

Kiva scrabbled backward until she hit the rear wall and could go no farther. Her hands went up in front of her, palms out, a barrier between her and whatever he was. "Stay away from me!"

Seth—or his ghost?—got up and crossed the space toward her.

She stared.

Death had changed him as it had her.

His dark eyes were bare of kohl. The black clothes covered his chest and arms and legs, as if to camouflage.

No. *Not* him. Not possible.

"You're dead." Kiva lowered her hands slightly. "I touched your *mummy*."

This Seth held out a hand. "Come on." His tone softened. "I'm not dead and neither are you."

She shrunk away from his hand. "Is this the afterlife?"

He squatted in front of her. "No, Kiva, it's not the afterlife. We're alive."

Kiva scrunched her eyes shut. "Then it has to be a dream, only a dream, it's—"

Seth pinched her arm.

"Ow!" Her eyes popped open and she rubbed the spot. "That *hurt*."

"It was supposed to. Now maybe you'll believe me. We are not dead, we are alive. This is not the afterlife, this is reality. Get over it and move on." He straightened back up and, again, offered his hand.

Kiva regarded it for a moment, then took hold.

Seth's hand felt solid and strong and as real as the pinch on her arm.

He yanked her to standing and then let go all in one motion, as if not being able to stand the contact with her for more than a second.

Kiva gasped. That definitely felt real.

He returned to his chair and gestured to his right. "Over there, water. Maybe you can drink enough to flush the cobwebs from your brain." He sighed impatiently.

Part of her wanted to run to him, to hug him, to tell him she was so glad that he wasn't dead.

But *that* Seth, the one in the chair? He wasn't the one she missed.

Maybe dreams, maybe death, were not supposed to be happy. But she was the sacrifice—why was she being punished?

Kiva wondered why he seemed to know so much about this dream. And why was he annoyed that she knew nothing?

She was almost afraid to ask, but she had to. "What is this place?"

Without looking at her, he held out his arms. "Welcome to the Tomb."

She didn't understand. She'd been in the tomb. With his body.

"But . . . I thought we weren't dead."

He swiveled around, then propped one bare foot up on the other chair. "We aren't. Far from it."

Afraid her legs might give out again at any moment, she tried to appear steady. "Are we in the palace?"

"No."

"Then are we under it?"

"No. Gods." Seth sighed again. "I told them they should have just let me go alone."

She persisted. "Go where?"

He dropped his foot and gestured at the chair. "You'd better sit for this."

Kiva complied, relieved to be off her shaky legs.

Seth walked over to the silver nozzle and held a shiny blue cup under it. Water poured out, automatic like the lights, stopping when he moved the cup away.

She couldn't help staring. "It's like everything is . . . is magic."

He rolled his eyes. "Not magic." He handed her the cup and plopped down in his chair. "Science."

"Science?" Kiva took a sip of the cold, refreshing water.

"Technology. You know all the stuff we learned in school about the future? Things they told us would be possible one day?"

Kiva nodded.

"Well, they lied about that." He gestured around them. "This is our present. Our *now*. Reality."

She scratched her head. "So, this *is* a dream?"

Seth smacked the heel of his hand against his forehead a few times and muttered, "Impossible." He leaned over the table in front of him and tapped the shiny surface. "If you won't listen to me, listen to your mom."

Suddenly, Sabra's face filled the table.

"Mom?" Kiva bent over and set a hand on her mother's face.

Instantly, Sabra began to speak. "Kiva, sweetie, I know you must be so confused—"

"Mom!" Kiva dropped her water and laid both palms on the screen. "I'm here. I'm alive."

Seth took Kiva's hands and whirled her toward him. "Are you kidding me? I know you're smarter than this. Can you listen?"

His face was inches from hers, his body so close.

Too close.

She shut her eyes.

Her other senses, dormant for so long, bloomed.

His scent.

She could do nothing other than breathe.

Mint and something else, something spicy. She inhaled deeper.

His hands on hers, so warm.

So concrete.

How did she feel to him? Smell to him?

Was she as real?

Seth spoke very slowly, as if she were a child. "Everything you know, about Alexandria . . . it's not real. It never was."

His words from the day of the quake came back to her.

Your world is as you see it to be. Until it isn't.

Her eyes opened.

Seth let go of her. "I have a lot to explain and it's going to be hard to understand." He leaned back, away from her.

She swallowed, unable to tear her gaze from his.

He tapped the table. "This is a computer. What you see is a video document, a vid-doc of your mom from yesterday. It's her, she is real, but she's not actually *here*."

Kiva didn't like being treated like a child. But she wanted to hear what her mom had to say. "I understand," she lied. "And I'm sorry I spilled my water."

"No biggie." He swiped a finger across the screen. "Ready?"

She nodded, even though she doubted she was ready for any of this.

"Take two." He picked up the cup and started the recording.

Kiva leaned forward to get a closer look. Gone was Sabra's glossy, dark hair. Layered, light brown hair barely reached her chin, and her blue eyes sparkled in a way the made-up ones never did. She wore the same simple black clothing that they did.

Sabra began, "I can only imagine what you are thinking, Kiva. This wasn't how I wanted you to find out, but our hands were forced. I know that for your whole life you thought you were in Alexandria, but that was not the case." She paused a moment. "You have never even stepped foot on Earth."

Kiva covered her mouth with a hand. What was she talking about? "Then where have I been?"

Seth brought more water and paused the recording. "She's not going to answer you."

"I know," snapped Kiva, wanting to understand and frustrated that she didn't. Her quivering hand took the cup.

Seth dropped into the other chair and glared at the screen before him.

Kiva chugged most of the water, trying to calm herself so she didn't break down in front of him.

What in the world was her mother talking about? How could she never have been on Earth?

"Do you need me to start it again?" Seth watched her.

"I can do it." Kiva gently touched her mother's frozen face. Nothing happened. "Mom?" She touched another place on the screen and garnered an identical result. She groaned.

Seth reached forward. "Swipe this way to—"

Kiva shoved his hand out of the way.

He frowned at her. "I can turn on the voice command if you want. But Hermione is annoying."

"Hermione?"

"I named the voice from an old book I read last year."

"Oh."

"Plus, it's way easier until you get the hang of it."

Get the hang of it?

She didn't want to be there *long enough* to get the hang of it.

She wanted to find out what was going on and how to get back home. She swiped her fingers along the tabletop and her mother resumed speaking.

Sabra sighed. "Sweetheart, this is going to seem impossible

to you, but please trust me. I was raised on Earth. In the United States, a place called Texas." She waved a hand in front of her face. "Never mind, Seth can show you maps and all that later. The point is, things on Earth went very, very wrong. I was twenty-two, going to college. It was the year 2037."

Kiva gasped.

The future. Her mother was from the future?

And that meant Seth was telling the truth. "I'm in the future?"

Seth tapped a small icon on the top of the screen. "Stop playback."

A calm but erudite female voice said, *"Stopping playback."*

Sabra's face froze once more.

"Is it too much?" asked Seth.

Kiva wanted to yell at him, but she didn't even know the words. Hearing the truth, if in fact that's what this was, had turned out to be exhausting. "I'm so confused."

Seth asked, "Well, do you want the quick and dirty from me? You can get all the details from your mom later?"

She had no idea which one of them she trusted less. Or from whom she would rather hear the inevitably disquieting dispatch.

Kiva drank the rest of her water, then went over and refilled the cup under the shiny spigot, so strange and yet almost familiar.

The truth was necessary. No matter how hard it would be for her to hear.

She returned to her chair and faced Seth, decisive. But as her head continued to clear, her mood seemed to darken in response. "So? Go ahead. You seem like you can't wait to tell me how much I *don't* know."

Seth rubbed his jaw, his confidence appearing ruffled. "I don't know where to start."

"What year is it?" asked Kiva.

Seth sat back in his chair. "I don't think that's the best place to—"

"Gods, Seth! Tell me what year it is."

"2053."

"No. No way." Kiva set the cup down before she spilled it again. "Not possible."

Seth shrugged. "You want me to lie?"

"Fine. Say I *do* believe that it's 2053." Kiva threw her arms out on either side. "Then where are we if we're not on Earth?"

Seth slumped a little in his chair and mumbled something.

She let her arms fall back to her lap. "What?"

He took a deep breath and leaned back, locking his hands behind his head. "There's not really an easy way to say it, so I'll just. . . . Do you remember when our teacher took us out at night to look at the stars?"

"She taught us about the planets and the solar system and—"

"And spoke about the future, how humans would one day build rockets to get them to the moon."

"I remember," said Kiva. "But it was fantasy, as much as when she told us about . . ." She glanced at the computer before her, and gazed around at the rest of the bridge.

Seth watched her a moment. "Yeah. So, the thing is . . . We're in space."

"Right." Kiva stood and began to pace. "It's 2053. And I'm in space." She stopped to stare at him. "Do I look that stupid?"

Seth got up. "Come with me."

"I'm not going anywhere." Kiva dropped into her chair. "*You're* dead. This is *my* dream. And I'm *tired*." She covered her face and groaned into her hands. "And, quite obviously, also losing my mind."

"No, you're not. You're fine."

She dropped her hands and raised her eyebrows.

"I can prove it." Seth gestured toward the door.

Kiva crossed her arms and glared up at him. "Why should I believe anything you say? If this is all technology, maybe you're just pretending to be someone that I . . . used to know."

"I'm not pretending."

Kiva raised her chin. "Prove it."

Seth sighed. "You have a cat named Sasha that likes to bring you mice, not always alive."

"That's not exactly a secret."

"Okay. How about . . . you love math?"

Kiva rolled her eyes. "Anyone could know that."

"True." Seth thought for a moment. "At your twelfth birthday party I gave you a stupid bracelet I made."

Kiva's hand brushed her empty wrist.

"And you kissed me on the cheek."

Kiva's eyes narrowed. No one knew that except her. And Seth.

"Kiva, I promise you. I'm not lying. I can prove it to you."

She didn't move.

"Don't you want to see the truth for yourself?"

Kiva stood. "Fine."

He headed for the door and she followed.

Kiva tried to keep up with Seth's long strides as they walked down the corridor. He turned a corner and stopped abruptly.

She ran into him and quickly stepped back.

"We're here." Seth pointed.

Goose bumps rose on Kiva's arms. A gasp bubbled up and out.

Before her lay floor to ceiling glass.

Beyond that, infinite blackness, prickled by the lights of millions of stars.

Kiva knelt before the window and pressed her forehead to the hard, cool surface. She found herself almost incapable of drawing a breath, never mind speaking.

Seth stood a few feet away, observing.

For several minutes Kiva stared out, barely blinking. Her shallow, ragged breaths fogged an imperfect circle on the glass. Finally, words came. "My mind is telling me not to believe it. But my eyes . . . We're . . . in *space*."

"We are."

Kiva flattened her hands on the glass. The stars were so close that she felt as if she could touch them. She cupped her hands around her eyes and narrowed her field of vision to include only the expanse of the universe. It was as if the floor fell away and she floated there, among the heavens.

Nothing had prepared her for that sight.

Or that feeling.

At last, she leaned back and dropped her hands, still staring out. Near the bottom left of the glass, she noticed a white ball. "What is that?"

"Earth. Home, technically." He added, "Not that we've ever been there."

"I still can't believe it." Kiva tore herself away and blinked at him. "We've really been up here, in space, our whole lives?"

He nodded. "On the *Krakatoa*."

"The what?"

"A high-tech airship. Only four of her kind." He noticed the blank look on her face. "They're actually a hybrid, with characteristics of blimps and advanced spacecraft. In order to have artificial gravity up here, there has to be rotation. The outside ring is designed to do that, but because the ship is so big, the rotation doesn't have to be that fast. You don't even notice it." He dropped to his knees beside her and peered out the glass. After a moment, he tapped on it. "There. See that?"

Amidst the twinkling stars, a light pulsed, too regular to be random. She squinted. "That tiny thing?"

He smiled. "The *Krakatoa* only looks small because we've been traveling away from her for nearly twelve hours."

Kiva stiffened. "Why are we traveling away? And what exactly are we on?"

His eyes met hers. "We're on the Tomb."

She raised her eyebrows.

He shrugged. "My nickname for it, given the circumstances. It's a shuttle, a smaller ship. The *Krakatoa* is made for orbiting more than traveling. It doesn't have the fuel capabilities for propulsion like this does, so it makes more sense to send this one."

"Does it rotate too?"

Seth shook his head. "The rotation would be way too fast. But it's small enough to have gravity plates in the walls and ceilings and floors."

Kiva's gaze turned back to the tiny light.

Was that really where she had grown up? Where her mother and Fai and all the others were now? Maybe her entire world had turned out to be fake, but the people never were. She needed to see them. Wanted to see them. Live in this reality alongside them. "I want to go back."

"We will." Seth seemed relaxed for the first time, as if getting her to understand their reality finally made him calm; at last, a peer with which to share the truth. "But they sent us on a mission. We have to do that first."

"What kind of mission? And why us?"

"Listen, there's a lot more I have to tell you."

Kiva felt his eyes on her.

Seth breathed out. "Maybe we should take small steps."

"Like showing me a million stars and telling me some tiny, blinking light is where I've lived my whole life?" If that was a small step, she didn't think she'd survive a big one. "Where in space are we?"

"Somewhere between Earth and Mars. You remember the planets?"

Kiva nodded. "I just never expected to be up among them."

Seth said, "Sorry you had to find out this way."

Kiva faced him. "How did *you* find out?"

He stretched out his legs and set his hands on the floor behind him. "When my mom died." Before Kiva had a chance to ask, he added, "Egypt seemed like our world, because it was. One made in virtual reality. I'll explain it all to you, or let your mom do it, but the real us, our bodies, have been in torpor chambers since we were little."

Kiva's forehead wrinkled. "And that means what?"

"While our minds were active, our bodies were in artificial hibernation. It cuts the food and water required, less waste."

"Were we always in the chambers?" Kiva asked.

Seth shook his head.

They sat there a moment, the only sound the hushed hum of the Tomb.

Kiva bit her lower lip. "It definitely seems easier to believe I'm in space when I'm actually looking at it." She sighed. "Tell me everything."

Seth shot her a glance. "You sure?"

"No." A corner of her mouth turned up.

He scratched his head. "Well, basically all the adults we know were raised on Earth, lived there until they had to leave."

Kiva sat down and leaned back against the glass. "What happened?"

"An asteroid was passing by Earth. Not near enough to do any damage, but it was part of a magnetic dust cloud, which hid a meteorite, Holocene, that hit the surface."

Kiva hugged her knees. "And then what?"

"Impact winter. Prolonged cold weather that was going to result in mass extinction."

"Wait." Kiva set her chin on her knees. "Everyone just left?"

"Not exactly." Seth stared out the window a moment. "For years before, the US government had been planning an evacuation—"

"To space?"

Seth nodded. "Geologists had been predicting the eruption of the super volcano under Yellowstone for a long time—" He noticed the glazed look in her eyes. "There are a lot of vid-docs you can watch." He started to get up.

"I'll watch them later."

Seth stopped.

"Please. Tell me the rest."

Seth settled back on his hands. "The US kept strategic preserves of oil in four underground salt domes."

"Like mines?"

"Exactly. Immense, secure spaces. The government decided they needed an exit strategy in case the super volcano did erupt, so they quietly hired a private space exploration company, Space Venture, to build the airships, one in each of the domes."

"People went into space on their own?" she asked.

"Well, rich ones did. Liam Trask was the billionaire that started Space Venture. And since the ships were ready when the meteorite hit, well, they were the first to leave."

Kiva glanced down at her wrist and the raised initials on the cuff. *SV*. One mystery solved. "They made these clothes."

"Space Venture outfitted everything on these ships. They had some pretty advanced stuff for the time that hadn't gone on the open market. Scientists had only speculated about high-tech airships, but Liam Trask actually built them." His tone had turned reverential.

"Is Trask your hero or something?"

"No." Seth wrinkled his nose. "These ships are impressive though. Everything on here can be accessed via voice command."

Kiva asked, "Can be?"

"I prefer manual." He smiled. "Hermione kind of freaks me out sometimes."

She agreed, even though she'd only heard the voice briefly. "Like she's trying to be human—"

"But isn't," he finished.

Their eyes met for a moment.

Kiva turned her attention back to outside. "They fit everyone in the United States on four ships?"

Seth didn't reply.

She glanced at him. "Did they?"

"Not even close." He rubbed his chin. "It was a lot of government officials and military. Scientists. The passengers of one ship, the *Tambora*, were chosen totally by Trask; that was in his contract. *Krakatoa* was mainly a mix of military and scientific experts. My dad was a general, my mom an engineer."

Kiva asked, "What was my mom?"

Seth hesitated a moment. "There were also some lucky ones."

"What does that mean?"

"The manifests for the four ships were decided long before the ships were ever ready. Higher-ups in the government and military. Scientists. Engineers. People capable of building a new civilization in space."

"Sounds to me like average citizens weren't invited," said Kiva.

Seth shook his head. "But when Holocene hit Earth, a lot of planning went out the window. Some of the people on the manifest were on board the ships, but many others had no chance of making it in time. And there were people not meant to be on board who . . . happened to be in the right place at the right time."

Kiva let that sink in. "But how did my mom get on?"

"I don't know. I only know she wasn't on the original manifest."

Her mother was only on the ship through random circumstances. Or serendipity. Were it not for chance, Kiva wouldn't even be alive. She didn't let herself dwell on that, there was more to know. "Where did the ships go when they left Earth?"

"The plan was to orbit Earth indefinitely, then eventually set course for a joint venture space station, Home Base, that several of the global powers had been building with the US." He paused. "Think of it like . . . a sky city."

Kiva tilted her head, trying to recall. "We learned about space stations in school, didn't we?"

Seth smiled. "You built that model with all the—"

"Cats. I got marked down for that."

"Duh. There could never be cats in space."

Kiva ran her hands through her hair. "Everything they told us would happen in the future . . . already existed?"

"Yeah. My mom developed the virtual reality program and they hooked all of us up when we were kids, after we entered torpor."

"How do I know this isn't part of that? How do you?" Kiva frowned and her words sped up. "We could still be in torpor and this could be another lie—"

Seth touched her knee. "Kiva, it isn't. You must know, somehow, that it isn't."

Kiva gazed back out at the stars. She didn't want Seth to be right. Thinking of her situation as not real was tempting. But her gut told her that this, no matter how hard to absorb, was real.

Seth took his hand away and sat there, as if waiting for her next question.

She had a million. "Why did they go through all the motions of school if it was stuff we didn't need to know?"

"But it *was* what we needed to know. They thought if all this technology was in our heads, then when we finally reached Home Base and were unsealed from torpor, the transition to the real world would be easy."

Kiva rolled her eyes. "They may want to work on that."

Seth smiled.

Kiva thought of something. "So why aren't we at the space station?"

"Home Base was supposed to be completed about ten years after the exodus from Earth. Other countries had ships as well. I don't know how many were able to evacuate after Holocene, or how many others are up here. But about six years in, they received word that it wouldn't be ready for at least another decade."

"Why not?"

Seth shrugged. "But that's when the leaders on *Krakatoa*

decided to utilize the torpor chambers in order to save resources."

"Like food?"

Seth nodded.

Kiva said, "Makes sense. That was when we were little?"

"Yeah. On our ship, about forty adults remained awake to tend everyone in the sleep chambers."

Kiva did a quick head count in her mind of all the citizens of Alexandria. With all the children and adults, maybe sixty in all. If all the adults were in on the ruse . . . "Why did they need so many people to care for, like, twenty people in torpor?"

Seth chewed the inside of his cheek for a moment. "There are over five hundred people in torpor on *Krakatoa*."

Kiva's mouth dropped open. Five hundred? "I've only known, like, forty people my whole life." She mused. "And it was all a dream."

"My mom worked hard to make it seem as real as possible."

Kiva's hand went for her wrist and found nothing. Once again, she'd forgotten that the bracelet was gone.

No, not simply gone.

If what Seth said was true, then the bracelet had never existed.

Kiva tried to reconcile the idea that her entire life had been a false existence, created by someone else. But she thought about the small things, minuscule details: the tiny legs of that scarab beetle, scrabbling in the air by the banks of the river. Her red bracelet, torn in half, lying in the rubble.

Her broken nail.

She spread out her fingers, all nails the same practical length, then eyed the pristine white walls, and behind her the sky full of stars.

Was she truly supposed to believe that this, something every child could picture in their heads, replicate easily with chalk on paper, was more authentic than Alexandria?

Seth leaned forward. "I swear." He placed a hand on hers. "This, right here? This is real."

A ripple ran up her arm.

Had she ever felt a thing as tangible as his touch?

He moved his hand away.

Kiva wanted to grab it back.

Maybe to prove she was still there, alive, and that this moment, the here and now with him, was the tiny ray of truth in an eclipse of lies.

Maybe she liked the way his touch felt.

Or maybe she was simply feeling sensory overload with the feelings and smells after years in torpor, and she craved more.

Seth sighed. "Anyway, it was a way for them to be with their kids, have a sort of life for part of the day."

"Everyone in torpor got to be in virtual reality?"

"If they wanted, but most stayed in solid torpor. Requires less. Plus, the years go by faster when you're in hibernation, which was appealing to most who didn't have a family on board. Or who had left their family behind."

"Why would someone leave their family?"

Seth said, "Holocene gave no advanced warning. People working on the ships didn't have time to get their families."

"Wait, so they left without them?"

Seth nodded.

"That is so sad." Kiva set a cheek on the cool glass. "Why did your mom choose ancient Egypt?"

"Everyone missed Earth. A lot. Living it every day in virtual reality would've been hard, knowing they couldn't ever have it back and that their own children would never experience that life. She considered it easier, and less depressing, to choose another time, another place. The ship's database had all the information and my mom created the program so we felt like we were actually in ancient Alexandria."

"But we never were," said Kiva.

"Our bodies never left the torpor chambers."

Kiva made a fist several times. "That's why my muscles feel so weird, so stiff."

"You've been out of the chamber for less than twenty-four hours."

Kiva noticed that he moved far easier than she did. "You seem to be doing pretty well."

Seth hesitated. "Other than brief visits, I've been out longer."

Kiva's jaw tightened. "How much longer?"

Seth didn't answer.

"You said you found out when your mom died. That was three years ago."

Seth looked down.

"Seth?"

He said nothing.

"How long have you been out of the torpor chamber?"

Seth stared outside.

"Tell me how long you've been awake."

He didn't answer.

To Kiva, it appeared as though he would remain silent. She wanted to know *exactly* how long he'd been living an actual life while she was stuck in some glass coffin like Snow White. She opened her mouth to prod him some more, but he cleared his throat.

Finally, he spoke. "When my mom died"—his eyes shifted down and he took a breath—"my dad realized that eventually they would have to tell us the truth. Me." His eyes flicked to her for a second. "You. The twins. Ada. We were the oldest of the generation born on the ship. We would need to know how to run it, tend the torpor chambers if something happened to the adults. So, he took me out of torpor and told me everything."

"When was this?" Kiva kept her eyes on him.

Seth avoided her eyes. "The day after my mom's funeral."

"That's why you didn't come back to school." Kiva sat up straight. "That's why we hardly ever saw you again."

"I went into virtual reality enough so you would all still keep believing it was real."

Kiva's face got hot. "You mean so we could keep living a lie." Her voice quavered. "They let *you* out and told *you* the truth. What about the rest of us?"

"It wasn't like that." As if attempting to show he cared, he held out a hand toward her.

Kiva leaned back, out of his reach. "You just left us there, in hibernation?"

"It was complicated. None of it was up to me. I couldn't—"

Her heartbeat raced. "You let us lie there like corpses? Thinking Alexandria was real and it wasn't?"

"You don't actually lie down; the torpor chambers are upright—"

"I don't care! It's the same thing."

Seth's eyes narrowed. "What, like it wasn't easy to figure out if you thought about it?" He snapped up his index finger. "We spoke English. *American* English." Middle finger joined the first. "Our teacher fed us virtual macaroni and cheese for lunch *every day* because she was too lazy to go on the computers and come up with an Egyptian food." Ring finger. "We had toothpaste and toothbrushes and deodorant and shampoo." Pinkie. "We studied Einstein's theories and he wasn't born until the nineteenth century!" He jabbed his thumb in the air. "Your mom read you bedtime stories. Pretty sure *The Wizard of Oz* wasn't around in ancient Egypt."

Kiva bit her lip.

Was he right?

How could she have known that she shouldn't have been aware of Snow White?

Seth pointed at her. "What's your favorite equation?"

"That's easy. Maxwell's. Although it's technically a set of equations." She clapped a hand over her mouth.

"Get it?" said Seth. "If Alexandria were real, you wouldn't even know what that was."

There were so many things that she couldn't have known if they were truly in Alexandria.

But there was no way for her to know which was which.

She thought Seth was being unfair to blame her for not knowing the difference.

He asked, "Should I go on?"

Kiva slapped his hand away. "It was real and we all believed it!" She pointed at him. "Even you."

"Once I knew the truth, it was so obvious."

"The truth was only obvious because you had the luxury of being out of torpor. You were able to compare the two."

"So many modern things didn't belong there. And we

talked like Americans, not Alexandrians!" Seth shook his head. "I still don't know how you and the others didn't figure it out."

Kiva's hand turned to fists. "How would I figure it out?" She was losing her breath. "It was the only world I ever knew. There was no other reality for me. How was I supposed to know what was or wasn't genuine?" She paused. "I believed that you were really dead." She left out the part about her grief; he didn't deserve to know how much she cared. "I even believed I was being sacrificed because of you."

"If it makes you feel any better, you were. That earthquake wasn't an earthquake. It was a debris field and it caused real damage to the *Krakatoa*."

Kiva frowned. "But they told us all that you died in the earthquake."

"They have to send me to another ship to get the part they need to fix the damage. And I didn't ever want to go back to Alexandria anyway, so they told everyone I died, had the funeral the next day—"

"What?" Kiva swallowed. "My mom told me over two months have passed."

Seth shook his head. "We hit the debris field day before yesterday. My so-called funeral was yesterday."

"I knew it." Kiva slumped. "Why did they make us all think it was seventy days?"

"To make the kids' belief in Alexandria even more solid."

Kiva had no words. Her gut clenched at the deception. And the lies that came straight from her mother.

"Anyway, they wouldn't let me go alone." Seth slammed his open hand onto the glass. "That's why we are both here."

Kiva watched him a moment. "You picked me to go along?"

"Ha. *Right*. You would have been my last choice."

Kiva bit her bottom lip. She was angry: angry at her mom for keeping her in the dark, angry at Seth for not caring that she knew nothing all that time. And those three years of frustration and hurt bubbled to the surface. "You were my best friend."

Seth got to his feet. "This is stupid. You can watch the vid-docs for answers. Just stay out of my way."

Kiva blurted, "You didn't once think to say, in all that time, 'Oh, maybe Kiva should know the truth too?'"

His shoulders tensed.

She hated her whiny tone, but there was no turning back, so she took a breath and reined it in. "You could have said that I needed to know how to run the ship too. That's something a best friend would do."

Seth simply stood there.

There *was* one thing only he could answer. "When did it happen, Seth?"

His forehead creased. "When did what happen?"

Her eyes locked on his. "When did you start hating me?"

Seth frowned, then opened his mouth as if to speak. Perhaps he wanted to defend himself, blame his coldness on his grief.

Maybe he was about to say that she was wrong, that he didn't hate her.

Or maybe he wasn't.

She didn't give him a chance. Kiva forced out a laugh. "This is fine, it really is."

Seth narrowed his eyes, as if debating whether to believe her or not.

"I'm good with it. You want to know what the best thing is about knowing that all that Egypt stuff was a complete and utter lie?" She got to her knees, then all the way up, barely a step away from him. She clenched her left fist tightly at her side.

Seth stiffened. "What?"

"It means you're not really a prince." She cocked her left arm and punched him in the face with everything she had.

The jolt sent a sharp rush of pain through her knuckles and wrist.

Seth staggered back, mouth hanging open as he held his hands over his right eye.

Kiva winced as she cradled her hand. "And you never *were.*" She stalked off down the corridor.

7

Back in the Tomb's control room or bridge or whatever the appropriate term—Kiva couldn't care less—she collapsed in what she decided to claim as her rightful chair. She was light-headed and her legs felt weak and her pulse raced from what she had just done.

Hitting Seth had been far from the best decision, but she didn't think she could have stopped herself. In fact, she knew she couldn't.

She gently massaged the knuckles of her left hand.

Every throb was worth it.

Without a word, Seth sat down in the other chair, one hand still over his eye. He swiped the other across the console in front of him and leaned over to scrutinize whatever was on the screen.

Kiva knew, deep down, that an apology would be the right thing to do. But after being so smug and mean, he had deserved it.

And she was, most definitely, not even close to being sorry. The ranks of liars would have to make do without her membership.

Her stomach rumbled. She slapped a hand over it, as if to silence her hunger.

"You should eat something."

Kiva didn't look at him. "I'm fine."

Seth's tone was didactic. "It's only a matter of time before you get light-headed."

Too late. "I'm *fine.*" She was tired of him telling her everything because she knew nothing. And she didn't want to rely on him, even if it meant starving.

He left.

"Good riddance." After two tries, she failed to get the recording of her mother going again. She tried to remember what Seth had said before to stop the playback. "Um, start playback?"

"Starting playback."

After several minutes of listening to her mother try to explain—more like defend—the deception, Kiva couldn't take it anymore. "Stop playback."

"Stopping playback."

She wanted to know the truth, the details, but not from one of those directly responsible for perpetrating the lies. Though no longer filled with terror and desperation, she suspected both the confusion and anger would hang around for a while.

But she needed some space, away from her mother.

Away from everyone.

She wanted to watch the Earth vid-docs that Seth had mentioned. Maybe they would tell her more about the background of her current reality than her mother, or Seth, ever could.

"Here." Seth set a red bowl in front of her, a silver fork stuck in a pile of pale, steaming noodles.

Kiva's mouth watered at the enticing, buttery smell. She held her face over the bowl and inhaled.

"Smells were the first thing I noticed too."

She glanced up at him and sucked in a breath at the sight of the skin around his right eye already bruising. A twinge of guilt popped into her gut.

He shrugged. "The virtual reality on *Krakatoa* was amazing. You could hear, see, touch, feel pain . . ."

Kiva's hand absently went to her shoulder, which had been injured in the earthquake, now completely fine. No wonder Fai had been so dismissive about her injury.

". . . but it lacked some things," continued Seth. "Like scents."

That explained why Kiva reacted so strongly to being close to him. He was the first person she had truly smelled. She leaned over the bowl of noodles, a close second in terms of gut reaction. She had to admit, he was kind to bring her food.

But she forced her hands still. "I'm not hungry." Her stomach rumbled, betraying her.

"Gods, you're stubborn. Just eat it."

She hesitated.

Seth dropped into his chair. "I know you're mad. But it's my job to make sure we stay alive, and food is part of it. As you're about to find out, taste is another area where virtual reality doesn't quite measure up."

He made the meal out of *obligation*?

Well, that should make the noodles taste *extra* good. Kiva swallowed her scorn, picked up the fork, and tentatively poked at them.

"They're freeze-dried and have to be reconstituted. Very processed. But not bad." Seth went back to whatever he was doing on his monitor.

The first bite proved to be blander than expected. But the act of eating, if not the taste itself, felt familiar, unlike anything else she'd experienced in the last half hour. And she had to admit, the real thing was far better than the apparently fake eating in Alexandria. And despite preferring to cease conversation with Seth, her questions were probably not going to be addressed by the vid-docs of Earth. "What did we eat in torpor?"

"We didn't." He pointed at her arm.

She stuck the fork in the noodles and rolled up her sleeve, revealing a bandage on her arm that seemed to start itching the moment she noticed it.

"Tubes gave us what we needed to stay alive. It'll heal fast." Seth pushed up the sleeve of his shirt, showing a faint scar.

Completely healed.

"Oh nice," spat Kiva. "Mine will look like that in, what would you say? About three years?"

Seth yanked his sleeve back down.

Kiva held the bowl up and began to eat with more gusto.

"You better slow down." Seth frowned. "Your digestive system was in torpor too. Might take a while to adjust to solid food."

Kiva ignored him and shoveled it in.

He sighed. "I'm trying to help here."

Kiva raised her eyebrows. "A little late, don't you think?" She pushed more noodles into her mouth.

Seth muttered, "Suit yourself."

The noodles were gone within minutes.

The warm, full feeling in her previously hollow belly vanquished any lingering doubt as to whether this was her reality or not. She sighed with contentment. Virtual life could not mimic a satisfying meal. "Can I watch those vid-docs you told me about?"

Seth pointed at the screen before her. "It's all on there."

She didn't feel like listening to Hermione again, so she tapped the icon in the hopes of deactivation.

Even though she had never touched an actual computer before, all of the motions of searching on it seemed familiar, in a fuzzy, déjà vu kind of way. If that had been the intent of their education in Alexandria, to prepare them for the day when they would return to the future, so to speak, then Kiva had to admit the adults had done well.

But moments after she began watching a vid-doc about plate tectonics and the super volcano under Yellowstone, her stomach gurgled. She inhaled sharply and set a hand over her mouth.

"You okay?" asked Seth.

She nodded, even though she was rapidly drifting far from the vicinity of okay. Her face was clammy, her throat felt full.

"You're going to be sick."

"No, I'm not—" But Kiva covered her mouth and ran for the door. Halfway there, she realized she didn't even know where she was running. Before she had a chance to decide on a destination, she doubled over and threw up.

Behind her, Seth groaned.

A lurch in her stomach buckled her knees. The rest of the noodles came up. She covered her nose at the stench of the puddle of sick and squeezed her eyes shut. "I'm sorry."

Seth said, "I did the same thing the first time I ate. And I know exactly how you feel right now, so I'm not going to say I told you so."

That didn't make her feel like any less of an idiot.

"You gonna be sick again?"

She shook her head. Her stomach was empty once more.

His hand touched her shoulder. Or maybe she imagined it.

"Might want to stick to liquid nutrition for a bit before you try solid food again."

Kiva nodded.

"Go lie down. I'll clean this up."

Kiva coughed. "No, I'll—"

Seth pulled her up by an arm. "There's a bathroom in your cabin. One excellent perk to space travel is that we make our own water and you can have a long, hot shower."

Kiva couldn't even look at him. She didn't want him to clean up her mess, but she also knew she was not capable of it. Grateful, she mumbled a thank-you.

"Hey. Kiva."

She paused, still facing away.

"I don't hate you."

He certainly had a funny way of showing it. Kiva blinked back tears.

"I never hated you. It's just . . ."

She mumbled, "I have to go," and quickly headed out the door for her cabin.

Kiva peeled up her shirt and wiped her face. "Don't you *dare* cry over him." She yanked the disgusting shirt over her head and tossed it aside. "Gods, I feel dirty."

In the bathroom, she leaned inside the shower.

Directly below the silver spout, a silver box dotted by black buttons was perched on the white-tiled wall.

A jab at the bottom button forced a rush of hot air at her from each corner of the stall, blowing her hair everywhere.

"Stop stop stop." A second push of that button stopped the flow.

Kiva shook her hair out of her eyes and leaned farther back, stretching her arm into the shower. She touched the top button and hopped back, managing to avoid the gush of hot water.

Within seconds, the small space had steamed up. She stripped, dropped the rest of her clothes on the floor, and stepped inside.

Kiva shut her eyes and moaned. "Perfect."

Nothing in her experience had ever felt quite as marvelous as that hot water pummeling her shoulders and back.

A memory flashed: Seth's hand on hers.

She did have to consider for a moment before dismissing it. "Not even close." Her words were tinny in the echoing space as she slowly spun, allowing the water to flow down her face and front.

Steeling herself, she pushed the second button from the top.

A pink substance oozed out and she caught some in her palm. "Oh." Shampoo like they'd had in Alexandria.

Except . . . She held it to her nose.

The smell was heavenly, sweet and fragrant. She knew, without knowing, that the scent belonged to some kind of flower.

Did she remember that from when she was a child? Before she was sealed away in torpor?

She lathered, piling her hair into a sudsy puff on top of her head.

The third mystery button turned out to be body cleanser, a green gel that emanated citrus as she soaped up and rinsed.

The heat sank into her skin and deeper still as it gradually loosened stiff muscles, unused until recently.

I am never getting out.

She was content to stand there for what seemed like hours.

Finally, when the skin on her fingertips shriveled, she turned off the water and stood there, dripping.

One touch of the bottom button and hot air enveloped her, drying her body, and even her long, thick hair, within moments.

Kiva left the shower and slid open the door of a cabinet right beside it. An eye-level shelf held an assortment of tubes and bottles. She opened one tube, took a bit on her finger, and touched it to her tongue. Again, she knew without knowing.

Another childhood remnant?

They'd had toothpaste in Alexandria, although it had been explained as a paste made from a plant that grew by the river and, miraculously, also had fibers that worked as floss. Apparently, they wanted them to learn dental hygiene in virtual reality, even if it wasn't exactly historically accurate.

She wondered how all of that worked in torpor. Something else to ask Seth.

"Now for clothes." Kiva kicked aside the worn garments, hoping for clean ones.

She swung open the doors of the cabinet by the bed and discovered stacks of shirts and pants and undergarments, exactly like she had just removed. "Yes." After getting dressed, she went back into the bathroom and brushed her teeth. She couldn't stop running her tongue over her smooth, clean teeth, a feeling she never remembered having in Alexandria.

No. Not Alexandria.

She needed to call it what it was. "Virtual reality."

Alexandria wasn't real, never had been.

In front of the mirror, she combed snarls from her curls. She winced at a particularly stubborn tangle and wondered why there seemed to be no technology to make that chore less painful. In virtual reality, her hair had been straight and glossy and no fuss.

She appraised her freckles.

Why hadn't she had them in Alexandria?

Seth had looked different there, and so had her mother. Of course, there had been dark eye makeup and clothing and jewelry, but there was more to it. They looked mostly the same, but . . . a better version of themselves.

Closer to perfect.

Kiva thought about it. No one had freckles or flaws in Alexandria. Fai had some wrinkles, but she was basically ancient.

Was it the virtual reality program? Were faultless replicas of people far simpler?

Kiva leaned closer to the mirror. The green of her eyes was nice. The freckles too. And she liked that her skin was a little darker than in virtual reality. She liked how her mom looked in real life as well: shorter hair and blue eyes without all that black stuff.

And Seth?

His longish hair and his dark eyes and skin made him look quite . . .

"Stop." No more caring or even *thinking* about Seth. Maybe they were stuck on that ship, but she would not let herself be dependent on him any more than she had to. The viddocs would teach her everything about her new reality . . . no . . . her *only* reality.

There would be no more feeling dense, no more being the one who had to keep asking questions.

After all, they'd sent her on this mission too.

Maybe she was the daughter of someone who wasn't even supposed to have survived Earth, but she would prove she deserved to be here, in this world. Plus, it was quite obvious that her mom had found her place as a contributing member of society. She could too.

Kiva straightened her shoulders and nodded at her reflection. "I'm going to learn how to run this ship if it's the last thing I do."

Her shoulders sagged.

Unfortunately, that meant going back out to the bridge and facing Seth, who had actually cleaned up after her.

That wouldn't be awkward at all.

She covered her face. "I can't believe I did that." Slowly,

she lowered her hands and stared at her reflection. "Doesn't matter. We're in space. We have a mission. And he's just going to have to deal with me." She tapped on the mirror. "Us. He's going to have to deal with us." She rolled her eyes. "Tomorrow. We'll wait until tomorrow."

The door whooshed open in the bedroom.

"You in here?" asked Seth.

"You could knock before you come in." She glanced at herself quickly, making sure everything was in place before she stepped out of the bathroom.

Seth stood by the open door. "Just checking to see if you're okay."

Kiva raised her eyebrows and crossed her arms.

He pointed at two buttons by the door. "Push the red for privacy. Green to open."

She hadn't seen those before. Another reason to feel ignorant.

"So? Feel better?"

How could she feel better with him there? She wanted him to leave, let her get her thoughts together, let her process everything that had happened. She nodded simply to make him leave.

He held out a thin device. "This can access all the same things as the large one on the bridge. You can watch the vid-docs about Earth. And there are others, about the ships, about everything. I thought you maybe wanted to stay in here." He paused. "Be alone. Or whatever."

Was he being *nice*? "Thanks."

He set it on the bed. "Just ask if you need help."

"I won't. Need help, I mean." Kiva didn't move, didn't uncross her arms.

"Okay. Well, my cabin is down the hall." He jabbed a thumb in the air. "Or I'll be on the bridge."

"Got it."

He left.

The door shut behind him.

She let out a deep breath and perched on the edge of the bed. She laid a hand on the device, still warm from his touch.

The door opened, Seth still there.

Kiva jerked her hand away and popped up.

He pointed at the button by the door. "You have to push the red for privacy."

"Got it."

He left and the door closed. Again.

She sprinted over and slammed her hand onto the red button, then set her back to the wall and slid down to the floor, holding her face in her hands. If every day out of torpor was going to be like this one, maybe she was going to have to figure out how to put herself back in.

Kiva sighed, gave herself a moment to regroup, then moved to the bed. With the small device in her lap, she started the first vid-doc, a tutorial of the United States. She took note of the state of Texas, which her mom had mentioned, and then moved on to Wyoming and Yellowstone and the super volcano.

She was motionless, enthralled by the visuals of the national park in normal times: stunning mountain vistas, herds of bison, roaming wolf packs, and thick, green forests. Geysers erupted, and turquoise and emerald pools of water steamed.

Then the facts began, about the super eruptions.

The Huckleberry Ridge eruption 2.1 million years before, the Mesa Falls eruption 1.3 million years, and later, the Lava Creek eruption. The three resulting calderas overlapped, and made up much of the land where Yellowstone sits.

The narration went on to describe the results of another super eruption. The ash cloud and spewing of sulfur dioxide would disrupt agriculture, clog rivers and streams.

Kiva stopped the vid-doc.

The nature was amazing, so different than Alexandria.

But she didn't want to hear more speculation, because that had apparently been convincing enough that the government prepared for a way out.

She chose another recording, which appeared to be completely about Space Venture, and its founder, Liam Trask. Other than brief footage of a tall, wiry man in a gray suit descending from the steps of a private jet, the billionaire himself did not speak. The piece strayed into gossip territory when it mentioned his messy divorce and the record settlement after a lengthy and nasty fight over a very valuable collection of emerald jewelry.

Kiva paused the vid-doc.

She wasn't exactly convinced that Trask seemed like someone an entire government would rely upon to save their citizens.

But, in the end, they hadn't saved all that many, had they?

The US government had never even planned to save the

general populace, only the people they could fit on four ships. People they deemed worthy of saving.

Kiva's pulse raced.

Her mother wasn't one of them.

Thus, neither was she.

There were so many questions.

How did her mother manage to get on board the *Krakatoa*? And if she had been born on the airship after it left Earth, then who was her father?

In all those years of Alexandria, virtual reality, she had never asked, there had never been a need. She had been told that her father was dead, died of a plague that also took many others. There was no reason to doubt her mother.

Since she was out of torpor, she wondered if her father was dead of a sickness on the *Krakatoa*, the story about the plague fitting their Egyptian reality.

But if the rest of her life was a lie, perhaps that was too?

Was her mother alone when she boarded the ship? Technically a stowaway, she required some sort of help, didn't she?

Was her father a passenger on the *Krakatoa*? Invited or not?

Kiva searched for her mother's vid-doc. "There you are." She leaned back against the lone pillow and tried to get comfortable. "What, Mr. Trask, you couldn't spring for more than one pillow?" She resumed playback.

Sabra began with apologies and explanations, then went back to the beginning. "I want to tell you my story. How I ended up on the *Krakatoa*." Her mother shifted in her chair and wiped her forehead.

"I was twenty-two, in grad school in Texas, assisting my geology professor with research for the summer. We were studying limestone near Big Hill." She shrugged. "I knew about the Strategic Petroleum Reserve. There are fourteen cavities, each one about two thousand feet in height, two hundred feet wide, each meant to hold about twelve million barrels of oil." Her eyes looked off to the left for a moment before returning to straight-ahead. "We were in this crappy little motel, and the housekeeper told me she saw trucks going in late at night now and then, hauling something other than oil."

Kiva whispered, "Space Venture. The *Krakatoa*."

Sabra scratched her nose. "I'd been obsessed with the NEO. Oh, you won't know what that is. Near Earth Object. The asteroid. I thought the near miss would be pretty cool." Her smile was forlorn. "Young and naive, I guess. Didn't realize how defenseless Earth really was when it came to the universe." She paused a moment. "Anyway, that weekend my professor had gone to Dallas for a conference. I'd met a marine named Jack who was working out at Big Hill. He was very tight-lipped about the job, but he asked me out and he was cute." She shrugged. "I said yes."

Kiva tried to picture her mother, not that many years older than she. On her own in Texas for the summer, with the freedom to do whatever she wanted with whomever she wanted.

Sabra squeezed her eyes shut for second. "I can't believe this is the first talk I have with you about dating. I mean, you're on a shuttle out in space, God knows where." She sighed. "We'll have a talk when you get back, I promise."

"Right." Dating, restaurants, the freedom to live on her own?

That was as much a part of Kiva's reality as dinosaurs.

That very moment, sitting in that cabin on the Tomb, was the first time she had truly been alone in her life.

The rest had been spent in torpor.

In Alexandria. A controlled life of studies, preparing for a future in space.

Her mother's life back on Earth? Her experiences?

Kiva would never come close to having them.

Her mother continued. "Sirens started going off during dessert." Her smile was forlorn. "Best—and last—tiramisu ever." Then she breathed out, long and harsh. "The NEO passed Earth by as expected. But the magnetic dust cloud surrounding it shrouded a meteorite. They barely had time to name it. Holocene turned out to be massive. Impact happened somewhere in Europe. Dust and ash were already blocking radiation from the sun. Global temperatures began to drop. Impact winter was inevitable."

Sabra stared off into space for a moment. "Jack drove us to Big Hill." She shook her head. "Crazy there. People running around. Jack took me right inside where . . . I can't even describe that first time I saw the *Krakatoa*. It was like a kind of blimp, but so huge." She smiled. "You'll have to find the schematics to fathom it."

Kiva frowned. Really? The Earth is crashing down around them and she's impressed by Trask's ship?

Her mother kept going. "Jack explained that the *Krakatoa* was in preparation for the super eruption, not some random meteorite. That's why it was so chaotic. They weren't ready." She swallowed. "Once we boarded, Jack left—"

The screen froze with Sabra's mouth half open, still speaking.

"What?" Kiva tapped on the computer. "No, come on." She pushed a few buttons, nothing happened. She tucked the computer under one arm and padded over to the door. She punched the green button and the panel slid open. "Be there . . ."

The floor pulsed beneath her feet on the way to the bridge, and as soon as the doors opened, the same cacophony as before assaulted her.

"What is that?" she yelled over the din.

Seth shut off the sound. "Music."

They had music in Alexandria. There was plenty of singing, and some of the adults made string instruments. "Not like any I've heard."

"Trust me, you haven't heard much." Seth turned it back on, but not as loud.

Again, the voices yelling.

Kiva shook her head. "But they're not even singing."

"They are. It's punk from the early part of the century."

She listened to the words for a moment. "They sound angry."

He shrugged. "Maybe I enjoy rage and discontent."

She smiled.

"There's a lot more music in the computer. Do you need something?"

Kiva sat down in her chair. "This froze. I can't get it to go again."

He tried a few things, then handed the device back. "It may have happened when she recorded it. She *was* in a hurry."

"I suppose." Kiva stared down at the device. "Can you find out the names of the original passengers on the *Krakatoa*?"

"I think so. Looking for anyone in particular?"

Kiva tightened her grip on the device. "Someone named Jack."

Seth frowned at her. "Why?"

Kiva met his gaze. "I think he may be my father."

Kiva anticipated that Seth would have some reason why she shouldn't look for her father. Or perhaps he was already aware of him; yet another item for the endless list of things he knew that she did not.

But her father was personal.

His truth was her truth.

Still, if Seth had any information . . .

"Do you know anything . . . about my father?"

Seth tapped his tabletop screen. "A little."

"And you didn't think I'd want to know?"

"You didn't ask until now. And like I said, I don't know

very much." Seth focused on the screen and slid his finger down. "Certainly not enough to make you happy."

She was annoyed that he might know *anything* about her father that she didn't. "Who is he?"

"I don't know who he is." His gaze lifted to hers. "But I might know where he is."

Kiva's heart pounded. "Did my mom tell you? Your dad?"

Seth straightened up in his chair. "The adults didn't tell me a lot."

Kiva narrowed her eyes. "No, just that our life was a lie and how to run the ship and—"

"Okay." Seth held up his hand. "Believe me, other than that, it wasn't exactly an intel open house. Conversations tended to stop when I showed up."

"Is my father alive? Is he—"

Seth crossed his arms.

Kiva forced herself to stay silent.

"When the four ships left Earth—"

Kiva bit her lip.

Seth sighed. "What? I can tell you want to say something."

"You mentioned the *Krakatoa* and *Tambora*. What were the others?"

Seth rattled off the names. "*Vesuvius* and *Pinatubo*. All volcanoes. Trask had a sense of humor, apparently." He raised his eyebrows.

"Got it. Go on."

"The four ships stayed together orbiting Earth for months. But then one was hit by orbital debris—"

"You mean like trash in space?" Kiva had to ask.

"Yeah. Like old satellites orbiting Earth at seventeen thousand miles per hour. Anyway, the ship tried to evade more of the mess and nearly collided with another ship. The president was still alive back then and realized the potential for a Kessler syndrome was too great." He stopped and raised an eyebrow.

She shook her head.

"Kessler syndrome is if there is enough debris in orbit that it all starts colliding and then causes a cascade—"

"Domino effect?"

Seth nodded. "All four ships could be taken out at once. The president ordered them out of orbit to give each a better chance of survival." Seth shifted in his chair. "They separated, tens of thousands of miles apart, all headed for Home Base."

"But I thought it wasn't ready yet."

"It wasn't. They set a very slow, steady course." He scratched his chin. "I guess, picture four swimmers all headed for the same shore. They're parallel, but far apart."

"And right now, you and I are going sideways, like from one swimmer to another."

He nodded.

"Things were fine after that?"

"I only know about *Krakatoa* for certain. Someone brought an illness on board that killed a dozen or so of the older people." He shrugged. "That's when the leadership shifted. My dad—"

"The Pharaoh?"

"The *General.* General Hawk." His words dripped with pride. "He set up a council. Picked your mom for it."

"Why? She wasn't even supposed to be on the ship."

Seth's forehead wrinkled a little. "Space can freak some people out. And others simply didn't make it to the launch in time." He shrugged. "There was room for smart individuals with ambition."

Kiva liked hearing that. She was proud of her mom for finding her place. "And my dad?"

"He maybe came up once."

"His name?"

Seth shook his head. "Your mom was talking to another adult and they didn't see me. The way she talked made it pretty clear she missed him, and more than just as a coworker."

"Missed him? So he is dead?"

"Not necessarily. Apparently, when the *Krakatoa* council found out that the space station wouldn't be ready for another decade, they slowed down the speed even more and—"

"They put everyone in torpor, you told me that." Her eyes widened. "Wait, is my dad in torpor?"

"No."

Kiva's shoulders slumped. That would have been so easy.

"But they were skeptical about the facts. The space station is a joint effort between several countries and a few private entities, including Space Venture. Since Trask hadn't always been forthright with the US government, a precedent for deception was there. They began to wonder if Home Base was actually complete and they were trying to prevent others from arriving."

Kiva frowned. "Why?"

Seth shrugged. "Wanted to keep it for themselves and their families? Who knows? Anyway, the *Krakatoa* council decided to send a shuttle to get more information."

Kiva glanced around. "Like this one?"

"Each of the airships has two." Seth leaned forward, elbows on his knees. "Kiva, your dad, or the man who might be your dad, went. Alone."

"He's on another ship?" She stood up. "On the space station?"

Seth glanced away, not meeting her eyes. "*Krakatoa* never heard from him again."

Kiva dropped back into the chair. "So, him being dead wasn't a lie after all." She stared down at the floor.

"You don't know that for sure." His tone was only somewhat patronizing, as if a small part of him believed in a possibility her father could be alive.

She asked, "What are the chances he's still out there somewhere? Wouldn't they have heard from him after all this time?"

"Not necessarily. Communications don't always work. The *Krakatoa* hasn't been in touch with the *Pinatubo* for nearly a decade, the other ships for at least a few years. Maybe someone heard from him."

Kiva wondered something. "How old was I when that happened?"

"I guess"—his forehead wrinkled—"we were probably around three or four."

"I must have known him." Kiva put a hand on her chest. "Until then, I knew my father."

"Do you remember him?"

"I don't." Tears welled up. "I don't remember him at all." She had lost her father again, before she even knew she had him.

Seth's tone was soft, almost kind. "Kiva, he could be out there. We don't know."

Tears spilled down one cheek. She smeared them away and stood up. "No, he's gone. That's fine." She grabbed the device and headed for the door.

"Wait," he called. "Do you still want to find out his name?"

She locked eyes with Seth, not caring that he could see how upset she was. "Does it even matter?"

"I . . ." His head tilted to the side a little. "I think that *I* would want to know."

Kiva felt a lump in her throat and more tears coming. "What good would it do?"

Seth looked down at his hands. "When my mom died, I was exactly like you. I had thought one thing my whole life, living in the palace, going to school. Having friends." His voice broke a little. "When she was gone and I found out that none of what I knew was true . . ." His eyes grew shiny. "I wanted to know who she was. Before the *Krakatoa*, before Alexandria. And it helped." He lifted and lowered a shoulder. "A little."

"But in the end, she's still gone." The words were sharper than Kiva intended. They also could not be taken back.

Seth glared at her. "Right." He shoved off with a foot and whirled his chair around, his back to her.

Kiva stood there a moment, then headed back to her cabin.

The events and emotions exacted their price, and Kiva fell asleep with another vid-doc still running. She woke up a little while later, pushed the device aside, and crawled under the covers, not emerging until she'd slept for several hours.

At some point during her slumber, the lights dimmed, but brightened again as soon as she stirred and began moving about. After a yawn and a stretch, she felt much more clearheaded than the last time she'd awoken.

Freshly brushed teeth and cold water splashed on her face gave her new resolve. She told her reflection, "Even if it doesn't matter, I want to know about my father."

On the bridge, Seth wasn't in sight.

Was he sleeping too?

What time was it, actually?

Did that even make a difference?

After being in torpor for years, her body might not even care if it was night or day. Was there even a night and day in space? Perhaps being awake and alert was all she could ask for.

"Good enough, anyway." She sat down in her chair and tapped the tabletop screen.

A plethora of options popped up. She managed to find the voice command switch. She said, "*Krakatoa* passengers" and waited.

Hermione, that strange, calm, voice again. *"Searching for* Krakatoa *manifest."* A few seconds later, a long list of names filled the screen. *"Manifest found. Manual or assist mode?"*

Kiva wasn't sure what that meant. "Assist?"

"Which passenger do you seek?"

Would this even work? "Jack."

"Searching for Jack." A few seconds passed. *"No Jack found."*

Kiva set her elbows on the console. Maybe Jack was a nickname. "All names that start with J."

In rapid-fire fashion, Hermione's voice announced several names, both of the first and last variety, all starting with *J*. None even sounded close to Jack.

"Stop!"

Hermione was silent.

Kiva leaned forward, chin in one hand. "What about Sabra?"

Hermione said, *"There is one."*

A visual of her mother filled the screen.

Kiva sighed. "I wish you were here to answer my questions."

Hermione responded, *"I can answer any question you like."*

Kiva muttered, "I didn't mean you." She deactivated the voice command before running a finger over her mother's face, which was instantly replaced by a series of other photos.

"Oh." Kiva scanned the thumbnails and touched the first.

A smiling, long-haired Sabra, in faded blue pants and a red top. Underneath the image, the words S. Stone.

"Sabra *Stone*?"

She swiped the image and another appeared. Her mother and several others. She recognized a younger Fai, as well as both of Seth's parents. All of their names appeared below.

F. Maxwell. N. Hawk. G. Hawk.

It was so strange to see the last names she never knew.

Was she Kiva Stone? Or was she something else? Her father's name, whatever it was?

The next photo was the same group, as was the next. She sped up and kept scrolling through photos. They were definitely from the early days on the *Krakatoa*, because her mother had long hair. Then they stopped.

"He has to be here." She swallowed.

Her mother hadn't spoken about Jack as someone she had known for a day and then forgotten. She spoke about him like he meant something to her. Like he meant a *lot* to her.

"Jack has to be my father." But why wasn't he in any of the images?

Kiva scrolled back through more slowly. She hadn't paid much attention to the additional photos of the core group of her mother and Seth's parents and Fai, but as she scrutinized more carefully on the second pass, one had an additional person, shown only in profile. A tall, handsome, dark-skinned man.

"And who are you?"

She found the new name below.

L. T. Kavajecz.

Without turning on the voice command, she keyed in the name. Nothing came up.

"And never mind."

"Good morning." Seth seemed upbeat as he sat down in the chair.

"Is it?"

"Good?" He tapped the console in front of him.

"Morning."

He glanced at her. "Yeah. Early though. Five or so."

"I only asked because no sun makes it hard to tell."

"That's my complaint about the shuttle. Not enough windows." He pulled up what looked like a map of the stars with a flashing green dot and a flashing blue one.

Kiva watched it for a moment. "What's that?"

He pointed at the green. "That's us. And the blue is *Vesuvius.*"

"One of the other ships?"

"Yes. That's where we're headed."

Kiva watched the dots for a moment. "How far away is it?"

"About three days."

"Do they know we're coming?"

Seth's hand froze, poised over the monitor. "Not exactly."

She sat back in her chair. "Wait. What's going to happen when we get there?"

"They're going to give us the part we need." Seth touched the screen. "Hopefully."

"What if they don't?"

He didn't answer.

"Well?" Kiva prodded. "Have you thought of that?"

"Yes!" Seth shot a glance her way, then focused on the screen again. "Of course we did."

We. Kiva scowled. How nice that he was part of the united front of adults, part of their leadership team. "Why didn't they just bring me out of torpor like they did with you? Why not just tell me everything that's going on?"

"There wasn't time. When the damage happened, they developed a plan to follow the authenticity of the virtual reality program and . . ."

"And what?" asked Kiva.

Seth stared at the screen.

"What?"

He set both hands on the tabletop. "My dad thought that if they did that, woke you up like they did me, that your mom would back out. She wouldn't let you go with me. He knew your mom was already worried that . . ."

Elbows on knees, Kiva leaned in. "Worried that what?"

"You wouldn't come back."

She frowned. "And your dad wasn't worried for you?"

"He didn't have a choice."

"He's the *leader.*" Kiva was confused. "Doesn't he make the final decisions?"

Seth swiveled the chair to face her. "Others on the

Krakatoa are getting frustrated. Restless. It's not good. Part of the council is threatening an insurrection."

"You mean like a mutiny?"

"Maybe."

"Oh." Kiva rested her chin on her hands.

Seth chewed on the inside of his cheek a moment. "When the damage to the ship happened, some of them forced my dad's hand. And a decision had to be made fast. The numbers are split, half are Manifesters, half aren't."

"What's a Manifester?"

"They believe that only the people originally intended to be on the ship, and their descendants, should be allowed to live on the space station."

Kiva frowned. "Do you believe that?"

"No, no way. Anyone who made it on one of those ships was meant to be here. I mean, that's fate, right? Or destiny? And I believe in destiny."

"And your dad? What does the general think?"

"He thinks the Manifesters are lunatics. We will need everyone to start this civilization once Home Base is ready."

Kiva asked, "So what happened?"

"None of them wanted to leave the *Krakatoa* and give the opposition an edge," said Seth. "So I volunteered to go."

Kiva raised her eyes to meet his. "But your dad didn't want you to."

He shook his head. "He definitely didn't want me to go alone. Not after what happened with your dad."

Kiva sat up. "So why did I get picked?"

"Your mom has been on my dad's side throughout the trouble. She agreed with him that I shouldn't go alone. But the ones mounting the insurrection—"

"Refused to go."

He nodded. "They told her to send her own daughter, which left my dad with no choice."

Kiva blew out a deep breath and leaned back in the chair. She remembered the overheard conversation between her mom and Fai that night. Fai had talked about dissenters. They must have been arguing about this.

He drummed his fingers on the tabletop. "I'm just worried about what's happened since we left." He stared down at the blinking lights on the screen but seemed to not really see them.

"You think they went through with the mutiny?"

"No way of knowing." He raised his hands over his head and stretched. "I can't dwell on that. We have a job to do. The sooner we get what we need, the sooner we can get back there."

Three days to their destination. Probably another three or four back. At least a week on the Tomb.

She wasn't about to sit there the whole time, watching vid-docs of the world that was. "I want to learn how to fly this thing."

"You don't exactly fly it." Seth didn't look at her. "Plus, I already know how."

Kiva frowned. "Well, what if something happens to you?"

"Like what?"

She thought a moment. "You could get sick."

"I feel fine."

Kiva mumbled, "Knife in the back, then."

The corner of his mouth turned up, just a little.

She was kidding. Mostly. "Do you really want me to sit here for the next week with nothing to do?"

"Suit yourself." Seth pointed at the screen in front of her. "Schematics of the ships and shuttles are on there."

She swiped until the file she sought popped up. There was no sense in messing around with the stupid Tomb, Seth would never let her take control. She rested her elbows on the tabletop and studied the schematics of the *Krakatoa* and her three sisters.

Fai had always taught her to begin at the small things. Once you understood those, you could move on, and the bigger things would make sense if you had the building blocks in place already.

Kiva started with what she considered the beginning: How did they keep the lights on?

Each ship had a primary power system: a radioisotope thermoelectric generator. The RTG was made of three parts:

thermal receptacle on the hull, the heat conversion unit, and the radioactive core. An RTG was capable of supplying 100 percent of the power needs, but had a short-term backup for worst-case scenarios. She studied the RTG for a little while, then asked Seth, "What needs to get fixed on the *Krakatoa*?"

Seth didn't look away from his own screen. "The heat conversion unit on the RTG."

"That's what converts the heat generated from the decay of the plutonium into electricity."

He glanced at her. "Right."

"There's no backup?"

He sat up. "They switched to backup power, but that's meant to be temporary. The HCU needs to be replaced."

"And the *Vesuvius* will have an extra one?"

Seth stared at his screen. "We don't know. The ships were supposed to have spares of everything, even the isotopes, but the *Krakatoa* had to launch before preparations were complete." He locked eyes with her. "We're banking on the *Vesuvius* having spare parts."

"And what if they don't want to share?"

Seth shook his head slightly, then went back to what he was doing.

Kiva returned to the schematics.

Each system—life support, heating, water, etc.—was controlled from the main bridge of the airship, on one main panel. One person, sitting in one position, had the capability at their fingertips to control the entire ship. "Trask was a genius."

Seth looked up. "*Is* a genius." He shrugged. "I think he's still out there on the *Tambora*."

Kiva kept reading.

Even small systems—referred to as subordinate in the schematics, such as the one that controlled the central vacuums in individual cabins—could be turned off and on from that single panel.

One sentence appeared at the bottom of every page, repeated over and over: WARNING: ONCE A SUBORDINATE SYSTEM IS POWERED DOWN, THERE IS A MANDATORY TEN-MINUTE DELAY BEFORE RESTART CAN OCCUR.

Kiva didn't know the purpose of the delay. Maybe to prevent a surge in power or something. Besides, all the subordinate systems weren't necessary to sustain life, so a delay probably didn't matter that much. She memorized the sequence to turn any of the systems off, then the sequence to restart.

Chances were she'd never need it, but having some kind of knowledge of her new world made her feel better.

Something cold touched her arm.

She jumped.

"Sorry." Seth held out a blue cup. "Breakfast?"

Kiva's hand immediately went to her stomach. "What is it?"

"Liquid nutrition. Very easy on the stomach."

She peered inside at the orange contents.

He said, "Mango flavored."

"Mango?"

"It's a fruit." He sipped his.

Kiva took a cautious sip. Fruity and smooth and refreshing. She took a bigger drink, mindful to not go too fast. "I like it."

"Good." Seth sounded sincere.

She wondered why he was being so nice. Especially after her cruel words. "I'm sorry for what I said last night. About your mom."

Seth shrugged. "You were right."

"It wasn't about being right. I shouldn't have said it."

He sat down and swiveled his chair toward her. "You were upset about your dad. I get it."

"Still. I'm sorry."

Seth pointed at her console. "How's that going? Ready to fly this thing yet?"

She swiped the screen blank before he could get a closer look. "Not quite." She took another drink. "Is the Tomb like the *Krakatoa*? I mean, in terms of how the systems work?"

Seth nodded. "Just on a smaller scale."

Kiva glanced around the bridge. "The main control panel is—"

Seth pointed at the tabletop in front of him. "Right here." He tilted his head at hers. "It could be set for that one. Or both. But this one can override that one. The shuttles are different from the big ships that way. I think this was meant to be used for training, eventually, and this is the instructor's seat."

Kiva was glad to hear that everything she learned about the *Krakatoa* would essentially apply to the operation of the Tomb. Because she did like the idea she could operate it if needed.

The shuttle jolted.

Kiva nearly dropped her cup. "What was that?"

"No idea." Seth swiped the screen. "I'll check systems." He bent low over the tabletop.

Kiva tried to see if he looked worried or not, then tapped her own screen until she got the map from earlier. She located them, the green flashing dot. But this time, a red dot was nearly next to it. "I thought the *Vesuvius* was three days away."

"It is." Seth kept working away at his console.

"Then why is this dot right next to us?"

"What?" Seth stood up and leaned over her, his midsection pressed against her shoulder. "That can't be right." He turned and headed for the door at a run.

Kiva set down her cup and followed. "What's going on?" Suddenly, the shuttle jolted to a stop so hard that Kiva fell forward and slammed her knees into the floor. She broke her fall, twisting one wrist. "Ow." She sat up and rubbed it, then got to her feet and continued running down the corridor. "Seth!" She rounded the corner.

Motionless, he stared out the glass wall.

She asked, "Are we stopped?"

Seth didn't answer.

The shuttle began moving again.

Kiva breathed out in relief. "Well, that's good."

But Seth muttered, "No. It's not."

She moved alongside him.

The stars were blocked by a massive, looming shape that set her pulse racing.

"We're moving again because we're in a tractor beam." He pointed outside. "And that? Is not *Vesuvius*."

10

Seth raced back to the bridge, Kiva at his heels. Breathless, she sat down in her chair.

He rapidly swiped and typed, his eyes half closed, jaw tight as he scanned whatever was on the screen. Then, suddenly, he sat back and set a hand over his eyes.

Kiva whispered, "Do you know what it is?"

He dropped his hand. "*Pinatubo*. One of the four ships."

"That's good, right?" Kiva sat up. "Maybe they have an extra HCU."

Seth did not seem to share her enthusiasm.

She asked him, "Why didn't we come to *Pinatubo* if it was closer?"

"Because we didn't know. The *Krakatoa* hasn't communicated with them for a very long time." Seth squeezed his bottom lip between two fingers.

Kiva's heart began to race. "Is there a chance my dad could be on that ship?"

"No way."

"Why not? Do you even know who is on that ship?"

"No, but—"

"Then don't." She jabbed a finger at him. "You do not get to tell me not to hope."

"Listen, your dad, if it even was your dad, left the *Krakatoa* on a shuttle and no one has heard from him since. There's no proof that he even made it to another ship."

Kiva glared at him. "Consider my hope dead and buried."

"Sorry, I just . . ." Seth stared at the screen. "I'm not saying he's dead, okay? I honestly don't think there's a chance that this is where he ended up."

"Fine. But what happens when we get there?" Kiva's heart raced. "Do we go say hello?"

Seth opened a drawer to his left and pulled out a knife. He secured it in the waistband of his pants and pulled his shirt down. "I go. You stay and hide."

"No chance." Kiva stood up.

"I don't know what I'm walking into." Seth got to his feet, towering over her as they stood chest to chest. "And I don't feel like having to save you."

"Well, maybe I don't need you to—" The shuttle jolted to a stop and she fell into him.

He caught her firmly. "I need you to go hide." He set his mouth at her ear, his breath warm on her skin. "Please, Keeves."

She froze.

She hadn't realized how much she missed being called that.

Face hot, she stepped back, unable to meet his gaze. "Fine. I'll hide."

"I'll be back." He set a hand briefly on her arm, then disappeared out the door.

Kiva wanted to follow him, go meet whoever might be out there. Maybe her dad, because she did still have hope he was alive, somewhere. But instead she kept her word and ran to her cabin. She hit the privacy switch to the door, then opened the cabinet. She climbed in the bottom and hugged her knees.

There, in the dark, her breaths were loud and shallow and fast. Her heart pounded so hard she felt it in her ears.

Seth seemed truly concerned about what he would find.

Who was on the *Pinatubo*?

Were they friendly?

What if they weren't?

Did they take Seth prisoner?

Would she be next?

As time crept along, the thoughts kept coming, fast and furious.

Why didn't she go with him?

Because Seth said he didn't want to have to save her.

And then he'd invoked his nickname for her, the one she thought she would never hear again. The sound of it, coming from him, had melted the ice still inside her.

She'd given in, believed that she needed him to protect her.

But how could he, if he didn't know what possible dangers might lay in store for them? She was not about to be a willing victim.

Kiva shoved open the door and crawled out. She ran to the bridge and yanked out the drawer where Seth had gotten the knife.

Another lay on top.

As she secured it in her own waistband the same way he had done, other contents of the drawer caught her eye. She lifted out a jumble of thick thread, white tangled with red.

BANG!

Kiva dropped the thread and shoved the drawer in, then raced back to her cabin. She settled herself in the cabinet, a tiny crack of light seeping through.

WHOOSH.

Kiva slapped a hand over her mouth.

How could she have forgotten to lock the door?

She managed to reach around to her back and get the knife.

Maybe they wouldn't look very hard.

pleasegoawaypleasegoawaypleasegoaway

Maybe, if they already had Seth, they would think he had been alone on the shuttle.

pleasegoawaypleasegoawaypleasegoaway

Her knuckles turned white around the knife.

She held her breath.

The cabinet flew open. A pair of unfamiliar black boots filled her view.

She screamed and jabbed the knife, hair falling into her eyes so she couldn't see.

Her attacker grunted and squeezed her wrist so hard it hurt.

She cried out and dropped the knife.

But then she threw a punch that connected with hard muscle.

"Hey!" Seth grabbed her arm. "It's me, it's me."

She swept hair out of her face.

His forehead wrinkled. "Are you okay?"

"No, I'm not okay! I didn't know what was happening and then I heard the door and then . . ." She looked up at him. "I could have stabbed you."

He let go of her. "Not likely."

"You scared me!"

He rubbed his stomach. "I'd say we're even."

She glanced at the doorway.

"I'm alone." He reached above her head to the top shelf, pulled down a pair of black boots like his, and dropped them at her feet. "Put these on."

"Why?" She held out a hand toward the door. "Is anyone on the ship?"

Seth tilted his head. "Come and see."

Kiva sat down and stared at the boots. "And what, they're just going to magically fit me?"

"The clothes fit, right?"

She glanced down at the pants and shirt.

"No magic," said Seth. "The *Krakatoa* has about any size there is, and your mom knew yours."

Kiva slipped her stockinged feet into the boots and stared at the laces. She had only ever worn sandals. She scowled. And technically, she'd never even worn those.

Seth knelt in front of her and tied the first. "They missed a few lessons in Alexandria."

She felt like a child as he tied and tightened the other.

He stood up. "Took me the better part of an afternoon to nail tying my stupid boots."

She wiggled her toes, which had a bit of extra room. Close enough. She took a few steps in the hard soles. Not especially comfortable, but she felt less vulnerable than when she only wore socks.

Seth asked, "Ready?"

Kiva picked up the knife and hesitated a moment before following.

Seth brushed his hand by the privacy button when he reached the door. "Apparently you need a refresher course on how to lock a—"

Kiva smacked him on the shoulder.

Seth grinned down at her. "Come on. You are about to see your first airship." He led her down the corridor away from the bridge.

"It's not really my first," Kiva said. "I mean, I was running around *Krukutou* before torpor, right?"

He didn't turn around. "Do you remember much about that?"

"No." She stared at his back as they walked. "Do you?"

He stopped abruptly.

She bumped into his back. "Sorry."

He faced her. "There are flashes from when I was little, I guess. They faded even more after I came out of torpor. Now the flashes . . . are of Alexandria."

"Do they ever stop?" she asked.

He raised his eyebrows. "I'll let you know."

She wondered what he saw in those memories.

He jabbed a thumb to his right. "Come on." The airlock,

a thick-bordered door, stood before them. "This is where the shuttle hooks up to the airship." Seth stepped over the high threshold and through.

She didn't follow.

He turned back. "Trust me, I already checked it out. It's safe."

Kiva still hesitated.

"I promise." Seth held out his hand.

Everything in her wanted to take hold. Not let go.

But did she need him to keep her safe?

No. At least, she hoped not.

Maybe he had a few extra years in the real world, but they had been raised the same. Whatever he could do, she should be able to do as well.

She simply needed time to prove that to him. And to herself.

Kiva secured the knife in her waistband, brushed past his outstretched hand, and entered the short passage to the airship *Pinatubo*.

Their footsteps clanged on the metal floor of the first long hallway.

Kiva let Seth go past her and followed him into a control room ten times the size of the one on the Tomb.

Kiva gazed at roughly a dozen black leather chairs and twice as many massive monitors that lay flat on the wall, not on tables like the Tomb. "Is it on autopilot?"

Seth sat down in the biggest chair near the center of the bank of monitors. "Yep, first thing I checked when I came on board. And still in a steady trajectory, from what I could figure out."

She sat in the chair nearest him, stiff leather creaking. "You didn't see anyone?"

"Nope."

"But someone must have activated the tractor beam, right?"

"Not necessarily. Except for the airship names painted on the outside, the shuttles for all the airships are identical, and a lot of things are automated. I think that when the Tomb came into range, the *Pinatubo* recognized it as one of her own shuttles returning home. The tractor beam automatically activated." Seth tapped the screen. "This is the main control panel. We can deactivate the tractor beam when we're ready to leave."

Tension left Kiva's shoulders.

They hadn't been caught in some nefarious spider's web after all. Just an automatic program. She made a mental note to check out that part of the schematics when she got back on the Tomb. "Where is everyone?"

"I don't know. But let's go find out." He stood up. "Feel like exploring?"

Kiva nodded. "Can we find the HCU we need?"

"We can look around, but it would be quicker to find

whoever is managing things. I'd love to ask them what they've heard from other ships. But first I want to check some other stuff out." Seth headed out the door and down a wide corridor. He acted as if he knew exactly where to go.

She walked fast to keep up. "Is this like the *Krakatoa*?"

"So far, identical." Seth pointed. "This way."

Kiva stopped in front of the biggest door panel she had ever seen. "What's in here?"

"If it's the same as *Krakatoa*, and I'd bet anything it is . . ." Seth pushed a button and the panel slid to the side. He breathed out. "Torpor chambers."

Kiva stared into the massive room that seemed never-ending, unable to keep her mouth from falling open.

A wide aisle stretched before them. Identical clear upright cases lined either side, each several inches taller than Seth. Each big enough to fit a fairly large human.

She became aware of Seth watching her and quickly closed her mouth. She wanted to stare, but she also didn't. Despite knowing the truth, she wasn't ready to see it. Not yet.

Her gaze drifted upward to the ceiling, which appeared to be at least forty feet over her head. She jumped when Seth touched her hand.

He said, "We can check out the rest of the ship."

Relieved, she followed him back into the corridor. "Where to?"

"This way." As they walked toward the end of the corridor, he said, "I want to see what they did with their Versa Space." They hit a T and he turned left.

"Their what?" Kiva glanced down the empty hallway to the right before following.

"Versa Space. Each of the ships is identical, but they were given some freedom. The people chosen for each were experts in their fields, geniuses."

She glanced at him. "Because they had to prepare for a life in space?"

"Exactly. But Trask was no slacker either. He wanted to make it possible for these great minds to keep discovering things, experimenting and inventing, even within the confines of the ship. He made sure each had a Versa Space, a gigantic room that they could use as they wanted."

"What's the Versa Space on the *Krakatoa* used for?" asked Kiva.

Seth took the next right. "It's where the virtual reality is set up. Our torpor chambers are in there, as well as the ones for our parents and the other adults who live in Alexandria. Much easier to monitor all of us, and unhook us from the VR if we're in one room."

"Do you know what other ships did with their Versa Space?"

"Nope." Seth stopped. "That's why I want to check it out." He pointed. "Right up here." The hallway ended in a sloping ramp that circled all the way up to what appeared to be another. "Race you!" He took off, running up the ramp, his boots clomping.

"Wait!" With a laugh, Kiva gave chase. How natural that felt. All those times they played tag as children. By the river instead of on a spaceship, but still. The familiarity sent a warmth all through her. But she was quickly out of breath and had to walk, still smiling when she reached Seth at the top.

"You're as slow as ever." He grinned.

Kiva bent over and set her hands on her knees, catching her breath. Was that the first time he had referenced their childhood? Their time together before all of this?

"Over here." Seth led her to a set of double doors, nearly identical to the ones on the hall of torpor chambers.

"What if it's something bad?" she asked.

His forehead wrinkled. "Why would it be bad?"

She glanced around. "What if it's why there isn't anyone here?"

"Relax." Seth set a hand on her arm. "I'm pretty sure most of them are in torpor. Just like on our ship."

She wanted to ask what would happen if they weren't, but he pushed open the doors and stepped inside. "Oh, no way!"

Kiva clapped a hand over her open mouth.

Seth threw both fists into the air, then turned to her, a huge grin on his face. "I hope you're hungry."

11

Kiva's eyes widened as she slowly rotated, unable to believe her eyes. She stood on a hill of grass, looking down at an orchard of fruit trees about seventy yards away.

Seth had run and already reached them. "Apples!" He plucked a juicy red one and bit into it. "Delicious!" He disappeared between the trunks.

"Wait!" Kiva tripped over her boots, then plopped down. She untied her boots and slipped off her socks. The grass was soft and warm under her bare feet. She walked in circles, her face up toward the sun. The sun! "How is this possible?"

Seth popped out from between the trees. "It's a greenhouse program, has to be!" He held the bottom of his shirt up, the resulting pouch a pile of red and yellow. "There are pears too!"

To their left lay a field of tall, amber stalks. Kiva pointed. "What's that?"

Seth turned. "I think it's wheat." He frowned.

She jogged closer to him. "What's wrong?"

"I just realized. If they have wheat, then they can make bread. And real noodles. This is amazing." He jogged up and dumped his find by Kiva's boots, then headed for the field.

Kiva followed him, striding slowly into the wheat. Her hands brushed the stiff stalks as the sun shone warm on her face. A breeze came up, blowing her hair out behind her. She stopped, closed her eyes, and held her face up to the light and warmth.

This reminded her of Alexandria, even though that hadn't been real. This, this was far closer to being so. She smiled. "I don't want to leave." Kiva opened her eyes.

Seth gazed at her, but not like he studied the console or a problem to be solved. He watched her as if . . . he liked what he saw. But he looked away. "We can't stay."

"I know." She sighed. "But this place is so . . ."

"Beautiful." He glanced at her when he said the word. He cleared his throat. "We should go."

"But why?" Kiva raised her arms to the sides. "We could gather more fruit." Something sparkled a short way beyond the wheat field. "Look!" She began to run toward it.

"Kiva! Wait!" Seth followed.

"Race you!" She pumped her arms, muscles responding like they'd been waiting for the exercise. As she got closer, she realized that the sparkle was the sun reflecting off a pristine lake. At the shore, she yanked the bottoms of her pants up to her knees, then splashed in. The refreshing water cooled her hot feet. She turned, laughing. "It feels wonderful!"

Seth stood on the bank, smiling at her.

"What?" She put her hands on her hips. "Do not even tell me to get out."

He sat down and unlaced his boots. Then he pulled his shirt off, splashed past her, and dove in. A few strong strokes sent him nearly to the middle, before he turned around and headed toward her.

"Don't get me wet!" She backpedaled, going deeper and getting wetter.

He stopped in front of her and stood up, dripping, a goofy smile on his face. He shook his head, drops from his hair splattering her.

She shrieked and covered her face, then dropped her hands. She grinned. "Where did you learn to swim?"

"The *Krakatoa*."

"There's a pool?"

Apparently done with the lake, Seth headed back to shore. He grabbed his shirt and wiped his face. "There's a lot of things on the *Krakatoa*."

A sudden chill sent goose bumps down Kiva's arms. She glanced skyward. A cloud passed over the sun.

"We really should go." Seth headed up the bank without waiting for her.

Kiva didn't get it.

One moment he was the Seth of old, her friend, someone she could actually stand to be around. But then, like a light, he switched back to the new Seth.

She started to wade out, but was still waist deep when her foot snagged on something below the surface. "Hey, wait. I'm caught on something."

Seth turned around.

Kicking didn't free her foot.

"Can you see what it is?" Seth sounded annoyed. "Probably some roots from the trees."

"No." She reached into the water and her hand brushed something soft and slimy. The cobras in the jar came to mind. She gasped and jerked her leg. Her foot didn't move, so her momentum sent her backward into the water.

Her head went under.

Kiva stood up, sputtering.

Seth laughed.

"Great." She coughed and spit out some water. "Thanks for the help."

"Hold on." He started back down the bank.

"Don't bother." She leaned over, foot still immobile under the surface. "I can do it myself."

"Fine." He sighed and sat down. "I'd like to leave sometime today, though."

She shivered.

Well, she was already wet. Might as well find out what she was caught on. She took a breath and plunged her head under the water, blinking until her vision cleared enough to see her foot.

A long, ragged end of a rope ensnared Kiva's ankle.

Thankfully, she didn't see anything slimy. Hopefully she could drag the rope ashore and cut herself free.

Kiva surfaced for a moment to catch her breath.

Seth was lying back on the grass, eyes shut.

Fine. She didn't need him anyway.

Mustering new determination, she yanked on the rope and reeled it closer. She took a quick breath and ducked back under, blinking until she could see clearly.

Next to her foot floated pale bloated hands, bound at the wrists by the other end of the rope.

She lurched and started to flee.

But the rope tightened and tripped her up. She fell sideways into the lake and found herself staring right into the dark, dull, sightless eyes of a corpse.

Kiva screamed, a silent yawn that filled her mouth and throat and lungs with water.

Hands grasped for any purchase.

Arms churned the water, trying to escape.

Her face surfaced for a second, enough to choke, but not enough to gasp any air before being dragged down again.

She kicked and splashed, inadvertently moving deeper, farther from salvation.

Suddenly, strong arms lifted her up out of the water and she coughed, spitting up water as she gasped for air.

"I've got you, Keeves." Seth carried her toward shore.

The rope around her ankle became taut, and dragged the body along in the water behind them.

Kiva wrapped her arms around his neck and held on as she hacked more water up and began to cry.

At the shore, he laid her on the grass, then grabbed the knife.

She squeezed her eyes shut, tears leaking out. "Please don't cut me!"

Seth sliced the rope and freed her foot.

Kiva lay there on the grass, her clothes and hair soaking wet.

On his knees, Seth leaned over her. "Are you okay?"

Still crying, she rolled her head from side to side. "I want to go. I want to go now."

"We will." He set a hand on her arm. "Wait here."

She sat up and wiped her eyes with the back of her wet hand. Useless.

He gaped at the corpse floating a few feet offshore, the rope drifting along beside it.

Kiva got to her feet and hugged herself. Her hands shook so hard that she made fists in an attempt to stop. Water dripped off her hair and down her back. She shivered.

Seth tried to block her view.

"Is it a man?" She started to move closer.

He held up a hand. "Just stay there."

Kiva swallowed. She didn't want to be frightened of everything in this new world. Not even death. She stepped closer.

He held his arm out to stop her going any farther, but she saw the dead man was bald and a little chubby. She asked, "How long do you think he's been dead?"

Seth wiped his knife on the grass. "I don't know."

She couldn't stop gawking. "Why was he tied up? Who did that?"

Seth took a step sideways so that he was directly in front of her. "We're leaving before we find out." He held her shoulders and turned her around, then gave her a slight push.

Seth grabbed their boots and let Kiva exit in front of him. Once they were out in the corridor, Seth shut the doors.

They were both breathing hard and dripping water onto the floor. He held out her socks and boots.

"Who do you think he was?"

"Doesn't matter." He pointed. "Get your boots on."

She sat down to put them on, wondering how to ask Seth to help tie them.

But he knelt before her to lace them up without being asked.

She watched him. "Thank you." She wasn't sure if she meant for tying her shoes or for freeing her from a dead body. She was grateful for both.

Seth said nothing as he tightened the lace on the second boot and scooted back to put his own back on.

Kiva pulled her drenched pants back down from where they were still rolled. "Do you think there are more bodies?"

Seth's gaze snapped to hers. "In the lake?"

Suddenly, she didn't want an answer. "Never mind."

He stood up. "Let's go."

They walked back down the circular ramp, neither in any mood to race as they had on the way up.

They took the same route back. He paused at the hall of torpor chambers and jabbed a thumb at the door. "We need to change. There should be extra clothes in here, it's a lot closer than running up to the private cabins."

Kiva kept walking. "I just want to go to my cabin."

Seth took her arm. "We're leaving our wet clothes here. I'm not taking any chances with what . . . might have been in that water."

She frowned. "Do you think he was sick? Did they tie him up and throw him in there because he was contagious?"

What if she had caught whatever it was, what if it was too late and—

"I don't think so. But dead bodies aren't exactly clean. We need to be cautious."

Kiva took a deep breath and followed Seth inside the hall of torpor chambers. She rubbed her hands together to try to get them to stop trembling.

"There must be some clothes in here." Seth walked farther into the massive space. "Be right back."

Kiva was too far away to see the contents of the chamber nearest her, but didn't want to stand there, cowering at the fate that belonged to these people, the same that befell her for the better part of her childhood. She gazed fully at the case before her.

The woman inside was a little shorter than she was, and naked but for strips of cloth wrapped across her chest and hip area. Kiva's face grew warm as she wondered if she'd been afforded that same scant amount of modesty all those years.

"Got lucky." Seth handed Kiva a stack of folded clothes and pointed at a chamber a few feet away. "You can go change behind there."

Eager to be rid of her wet clothes and anything that may have brushed up against the corpse, she found her hiding spot and quickly stripped, yanking the pants down over the boots. This place made her nervous and she didn't like being alone.

The underthings were a little big, but they'd do for the moment. "So how do these things work? The chambers?"

From the sound of his voice, Seth wasn't very far away. "Each has a small control panel up at the top that basically monitors their vital signs. You can tell with a glance if everything is okay or not."

Kiva sat down. Getting the clean, dry pants on over the boots took some muscle, but she managed. When she was in the new clothes, she ran her fingers through her damp hair, trying to get out some tangles as best she could. Then she stepped back out.

Seth stood a few feet away, also in dry clothes. His wet hair hung loose to his shoulders.

She asked, "How can you tell with a glance that everything is fine?"

He pointed at a small screen at the top of the case, and a button beside it. "You push that and it flashes green."

"They only flash green?"

"No. Also yellow."

"What's yellow mean?" she asked.

"There's a problem." Seth added, "And if it's red . . ."

Kiva frowned. "Worse problem?"

"Much. Red is . . . dead."

Kiva shivered. "So that's why they don't need that many people to watch over the people in torpor."

"Yeah. Once you're used to it, you can check about ten,

fifteen people in a couple of minutes." Seth knocked on the front of the case. "Pretty efficient."

Kiva stared. The woman appeared to be asleep, a look of peace on her face. "Is she in virtual reality?"

"I don't think anyone else besides my mom came up with the program. And since their Versa Space is the orchard and the"—he seemed about to say *lake*, but instead simply added—"my guess is no."

Kiva stepped closer, then her gaze went down the row. "How many people are in this place?"

Seth went a few yards down the aisle. "I'd say at least four hundred. Maybe more. Definitely not all."

"How do you know?"

"I just do."

Kiva brushed past him and meandered a bit more. She passed dozens of the cases, dozens of faces, all like the woman. Sleeping. Peaceful.

She scrunched her eyes shut and imagined herself in torpor, next to Ada and Rem and Rom in their own cases.

How could Seth have seen them, day after day, and not wanted to let them out?

She opened her eyes. "How hard is it to bring someone out of it?"

"Easy, actually. You just have to choose the awakening protocol on the panel and —" Seth came closer. "I wouldn't try it if I were you."

She glared at him. "I meant *me.* How hard was it?"

He looked away. "I wasn't there."

"But was it? I mean, it must have been difficult, right? Otherwise, it seems to me that you might have tried."

He set a hand on his forehead and shut his eyes. "Gods, we have to go, Kiva. Don't start this—"

"Start what?" Kiva set her hands on her hips. "You tell me how easy it is to take care of all these people, how simple everything is, but you can't manage to let me out?" She marched over to one of the cases and stared at the man inside, dark beard reaching nearly to his chest. "Should we see how hard it is to free this guy?"

Seth frowned. "It's not funny."

"What? I push the button, right?" She held her hand up.

"Kiva, don't!"

Kiva pushed the button. The screen flashed red.

Her hand froze in midair.

Red meant . . .

Seth pushed her out of the way. "Wait over there."

"What did I do?" Kiva gulped. "Seth, what did I do?"

He grabbed her arm. "Wait. Over. There."

She backed off, heart pounding.

"Come on." Seth tapped the panel. "It's just a glitch." He hammered on the panel with a fist. "Has to be."

Kiva finally tore her gaze off the man's face and turned around.

More faces.

She twirled in another direction.

More.

Dozens of faces within feet of her, no matter which way she turned.

Was this a ship of death? Was *nobody* alive?

She had to know, she had to know that they weren't corpses floating in the glass. She had to know that they weren't dead too.

The closest chamber was a foot away. *Please be green.* She tapped the panel.

Red.

She walked to the next. *Green, please please please.*

Tap.

Red.

The next.

Tap.

Red.

"No."

The next and the next.

Tap tap.

Red, red.

"No. No."

The next and the next and the next . . .

Tap tap tap . . .

Red red red . . .

"No. No. No."

Red meant . . .

Dead.

She screamed.

"Kiva!" Seth was there, in her face. "Come on. Stop."

"They're dead!" She sobbed. "Everyone on this ship is dead!"

Seth crushed her face to his chest, his hold so tight she couldn't move.

"They're all dead." Her words were muffled.

He cradled her head with one hand and murmured in her ear, "Keeves, it's a mistake. They can't be dead. Not all of them."

"The boy is right."

Seth released her and whirled around.

Kiva gasped at the thin man in thick, black-framed glasses who blocked their exit.

His clothing matched theirs, but his face was pale, and his hair jet-black with streaks of gray. "They're not *all* dead." Behind the glasses his dark eyes appeared to enlarge like a bug's. "Just the ones I didn't like very much."

12

Kiva reached a trembling hand out for Seth.

He grabbed hold, shoved her behind him, and set his legs in a wide stance. With his shoulders raised and jaw lowered, he asked the man, "Who are you?"

"Stand down, son." The man's smile was yellowed and gap-toothed. "I'm kidding, kidding." He pointed at the red-screened chambers. "Those unfortunate souls *are* dead. But through their own actions."

Kiva peered around Seth.

He hissed, "Stay back."

"No need to be afraid, girlie." The man held up both

palms. "I surrender!" He cackled. "Tell your boyfriend here that he has nothing to worry about."

"He's not my boyfriend." Kiva moved even with Seth.

He jutted out an elbow to keep her behind him, one hand an inch from his concealed knife.

"Welcome to the *Pinatubo*. I'm Felix Kubota, PhD."

"I'm Seth Hawk."

Kiva glanced up at Seth. She knew he had two names, but she'd never heard them spoken aloud before.

"Hawk." The man tilted his head. "I knew a General Hawk when this project started."

"He's my father," said Seth.

"You don't say!" The man clapped his hands. "That makes you a descendant of one of the True."

Seth frowned. "The True?"

"The people on the original manifest of the four ships. The ones meant to leave Earth, start a new civilization in space." Kubota regarded Kiva. "And you are?"

Seth blurted out, "Kiva Maxwell."

Her gaze slid sideways. Fai's last name. Why?

"Maxwell . . . ," mused Kubota. "My favorite set of equations."

"Mine too," blurted Kiva.

The man's gaze slid to her. "How convenient."

Seth added, "Dr. Fai Maxwell is her mother, on the original manifest if you care to check."

"Oh, no need, no need. I'll take your word for it." Kubota rubbed his hands together, as if eager. "So, not only do I have the pleasure of visitors, but they turn out to be True. This is indeed a good day." He held a hand out to his side. "And now, if you care to follow me, I will prepare us a repast and we can get to know one another." With a pronounced limp, the man left the room.

Kiva whispered to Seth, "Why did you tell him that's my name?"

"Better that he thinks we're both meant to be on the *Krakatoa*."

"Why?"

His eyebrows slanted down. "Because he's obviously on the side of the Manifesters. Better he thinks you're meant to be here. So please, just go with it for now."

"Fine."

Seth headed toward the door.

Kiva shot a glance at the row of dead people and followed.

Kubota waited for them in the corridor. "You seem a bit damp."

Seth said, "We wanted to see if it was like the *Krakatoa*. There was . . . rain in the Versa Space."

"The rain is my doing," said Kubota. "One of my personal projects on Earth was an artificial weather prototype for use in drought-ravaged areas. I was able to successfully implement it on a small scale in the Versa Space." He raised his arms out to the side. "This place looks very familiar to you both, I assume?"

"Yes." Seth poked Kiva's side.

"Yes, for sure," she said. "I feel very much at home."

Kubota turned his back to them.

Seth scowled and raised his palms up at her.

She shrugged and followed their host.

Kubota barely moved faster than a crawl down the hallway. "Now what brings you out to my neck of the universe?"

Seth said, "We need to replace the HCU."

Kubota stopped and faced him. "Young man, you are in luck." He bowed to Kiva. "And young lady." He straightened back up. "We will collect that before our refreshments."

Kiva widened her eyes at Seth, who shrugged but had a hopeful look on his face. Maybe they wouldn't have to go any farther, and could return home sooner than planned. Although Kiva realized that would mean abandoning the search for her father.

Seth said, "We had hoped one of the ships might have a spare HCU. But don't you need to keep it?"

Kubota's snail pace continued. "Do you know anything about the power systems on these ships?"

Kiva said, "One primary source, the RTG."

Kubota stopped and faced them. "Yes. Do you know anything about the radioactive isotope?"

Seth said, "Basically, it'll last forever?"

"*It'll last forever.* You sound like my last supervisor." Dr. Kubota shuffled forward again, taking a right at the T. "Let me tell you an old joke. The engineer says to whoever is paying for the job: How do you want it done? On *time*? On *budget?* Or *correctly*?" He held up two fingers. "Choose two." He cackled.

Kiva and Seth looked at each other.

"I helped design the RTGs on these ships. Trask headhunted me from Google." He stopped. "Big company? You've heard of it?"

They shook their heads.

"You should google it some time." He cackled again and kept moving. "There were two approaches for power on these ships that we designed. Build many small systems that would, of course, be expected to not all be working at once. But they are easily repaired or replaced. Or, you go with one big system that can't possibly fail." He paused. "Until it does."

A long, four-wheeled cart sat at the side of the hallway. He pointed. "Bring that, will you?"

Seth pushed. The wheels screeched.

"Oh my, I need some oil." Kubota led the way another ten yards. "For the first time in my life as a physicist, my ideas aren't being squashed for not being financially feasible. I've made a lot of headway on my antigravity propulsion and atmosphere reentry experiments." He opened a door on the left. The room was full of boxes and bins and barrels, all labeled SPACE VENTURE. He pushed aside a few boxes. "Somewhere . . ." He pointed at a wooden crate. "There!"

Seth maneuvered the screeching cart as close as possible. The three of them managed to lift the heavy load onto the cart. Kiva wondered how they were going to carry it through the airlock.

They headed back the way they came, wheels announcing them the entire way. Kubota pointed at a door they'd passed before. "Now for some refreshments."

Kiva entered the space, so large that close to a dozen long tables stretched down the length of it, plenty of space between each.

Kubota pointed to a small round table with four chairs at the side of the hall. "That's become my lunch table. Wait there."

Kiva sat down in a metal chair.

"Do you need any help, Dr. Kubota?" asked Seth.

"Please, call me Felix." The man waved him off. "No, no. I'm happy to have someone to serve beside myself. And Cleo, of course."

Seth and Kiva exchanged a glance. She asked, "Cleo?"

Kubota stopped. "I didn't mention Cleo?"

Kiva shook her head.

"Well, wait here. I will go find her." Kubota limped off.

Seth sat down. "I didn't expect a big crew to be awake, but it makes no sense that he is the *only one*."

"He's not," said Kiva. "There's Cleo."

"For all we know, she could be imaginary." Seth leaned in closer to her. "We need to leave as soon as we can."

She hoped he had a plan, because they weren't exactly going to sneak out of there with the HCU.

"Here we are!" Kubota carried something black and furry in his arms. "Meet my stalwart companion."

"A cat!" Kiva turned to Seth. "I knew there could be cats in space."

Kubota smiled, apparently very pleased at her reaction. "A friend of felines, I can tell." He set Cleo in Kiva's arms.

Kiva stroked her sleek fur. "I have a cat." Then she realized that she didn't. Sasha had never existed. "I mean, I—"

Seth kicked her under the table.

She glared at him.

"What happened to your cat?" Kubota sat down.

"She died," said Seth. "It was sad."

The man nodded his head. "Yes, of course it was."

Ignoring Seth, Kiva asked, "Where did Cleo come from?"

"One of the original passengers brought a pair on board." Kubota lowered his voice. "Not one of the True, believe me. The True knew better. They were aware of the protocols to be followed." His voice returned to a normal level. "But who doesn't like cats? Even I couldn't bear them any ill will, despite the deception that accounted for their presence. Several batches of kittens were born over the years." He rubbed the cat's ears. "Cleo here is from the last. She's over a decade old."

"Ten years?" asked Kiva. "Is that old for a cat?"

"Not terribly." The man's focus seemed to drift. "I remember when my Casey was ten. Seems like yesterday."

"You have children?" asked Seth.

Kubota snapped out of it. "Where was I? Oh yes. Snacks." He got to his feet and shambled out a door at the side of the room.

Kiva continued to stroke Cleo. "I can't believe I'm holding a real cat."

"You need to tone it down," said Seth.

"Seriously?" She stared at him. "Why wouldn't I be excited about a cat?"

Seth lowered his voice. "Just be careful what you say. There are dead people in there."

"He said it wasn't because of him," said Kiva.

Seth's eyes narrowed. "And you believe him?"

"He's giving us the part we need." She shrugged. "That's good enough for me."

Seth said, "Kiva, did you forget? Your foot was caught on a dead man in the lake."

Her skin crawled. "Of course not!"

Seth set a finger to his lips. "Please, just let's be careful, okay? My dad will want to know what happened here, but Kubota seems to have an agenda."

"That True stuff?" Kiva frowned. "Does it really matter who was meant to be on the ships and who ended up on them?"

Seth leaned closer to Kiva. "Clearly it does to him and the Manifesters. Don't tell him or anyone else we may meet that your mom wasn't on the original manifest."

Kiva took a deep breath and concentrated on the warmth and steady purring that emanated from Cleo.

"Do you think Kubota feels strongly enough—"

"To act on it?" Seth shook his head. "I do not want to hang around long enough to find out. Whatever you do, steer away from talking about the dead people, okay?"

"No problem there." Kiva preferred not to know the answers to any of the questions currently racing around her head.

"Well, here we are!" Kubota returned bearing a large tray laden with a silver teapot, three cups, a small bowl, and a plate of thin, brownish cookies.

"I'll get that." Seth jumped up and took the tray, then set it on the table. They both sat down.

"Cleo is not welcome at the table when we eat. We at least keep a pretense of civility around here." Kubota snapped his fingers. "Kitty. Down."

The cat stretched in Kiva's lap, then jumped to the floor

and padded over to a nearby table. She sat down under it and proceeded to lick her paw and wipe it across her face.

Kiva tried to keep her words light and normal. "She's lovely."

"So is my coffee." Dr. Kubota poured three cups and held up the bowl, which was piled with sparkling white cubes.

"You've got sugar?" Seth made no effort to hide his surprise and ignored Kiva's subsequent glare.

Their host smiled. "You'd be amazed what I have squirreled away. Of course, it also helped that nearly all of the passengers went into torpor within a year of launch."

Seth's eyes widened. "They've been under the whole time?"

Kubota nodded. "Most of them. Except for those of us who monitor the sleeping."

Kiva glanced around. "Is someone else here? You're not the only one awake?"

"Oh, now I am." The man blew on his coffee. "I wasn't always." He pushed the plate toward Seth. "Eat, eat. These are special occasion cookies."

Seth bit into one and smiled. "That's good."

"Cinnamon and molasses. I make the flour myself from the wheat. You were in the Versa Room long enough to see the wheat field, I take it?"

Kiva shot Seth a glance, but he gave his full attention to his cookie.

Did Kubota suspect they saw the body?

"And you, my dear." Kubota pushed the plate toward Kiva.

Though the mere thought of solid food made her stomach flip, something told her that refusing the cookies and insulting their host would be a mistake. She took one. "Looks delicious." But as soon as the man turned to Seth, she stuffed the cookie up her sleeve and feigned chewing when he glanced back her way.

"So, to answer your question, Seth, we monitored the sleeping in pairs of two. Shifts of six months." Kubota took a sip from his cup. "My first shift was a year into the voyage. I'd been in torpor since early into the voyage, as I said earlier. I didn't really have a chance to deal with everything that had happened."

"It must have been horrible, to have to leave Earth like that." Seth dunked another cookie in his coffee before stuffing it in his mouth.

"Yes, yes. Horrible is the word." Kubota stared at the table, seeming to lose focus, the same as earlier.

Kiva said, "My mother told me that everything happened so fast."

Seth's hand froze midair as he reached for another cookie. He widened his eyes and shook his head at Kiva.

But she kept talking. "She said the launch was very chaotic."

“Chaotic?” Kubota snapped out of his reverie and stared at her, eyes narrowing. “That’s what she said?”

Kiva gulped. “Yes sir.” The words were whispered.

“Chaotic is not the word I would choose.” With a grunt, he heaved his cup toward the closest wall, where it shattered on impact and coffee dripped down in long, brown trails.

Kiva held her breath. She couldn’t even look at Seth.

“Tell me.” The man set his elbows on the table. His eyes turned to slits. “Was that chaotic?”

13

Kiva held her breath. She didn't know how to respond.

Dr. Kubota said, "Allow me to answer. Perhaps frightening? Alarming? Dreadful? Harrowing? Traumatic—"

"We weren't even born yet," interrupted Seth. "Forgive us, but we have no way of understanding how terrible it was for all of you."

"Unspeakable." Kubota's gaze drifted to him.

Kiva exhaled slowly, grateful to Seth for turning the man's attention away from her.

Kubota pushed the plate between the two of them. "You eat your cookies and I'll tell you exactly what it was like. So perhaps you may understand a bit better."

Seth took two more and Kiva one. She pretended to eat and hoped she was convincing enough.

Kubota pushed his glasses up using one finger on the nosepiece. "I'd been on the airship project for nearly seven years. I was able to do my engineering from home half of each month. I lived with my family in California." He stopped.

Kiva felt like he was waiting for them to say something. She took a chance. "Your family?"

"My wife, Angie. My daughter, Casey. We celebrated her tenth birthday the night before I flew back to the ship's construction site at a salt dome in Louisiana. She and I went up on the balcony and watched the NEO through the telescope." His eyes glittered. "She wanted to go into space more than anything. I almost told her about my work that night."

He took a handkerchief out of his sleeve and wiped his eyes. "The airship project was a secret. But we were on the manifest. My family and I had space on the *Pinatubo* whenever it was time to evacuate Earth. My Casey would get to live in space."

Kiva's stomach clenched more and more as the man kept rambling. She wanted so badly to look at Seth, but didn't want Kubota to notice and possibly take offense. He was a powder keg simply waiting for a match.

"I had a bad feeling that day." Kubota poured more coffee for Seth, who had managed to drain his cup. "We were on the ship when sirens went off. The launch code started." He dropped his head into his hands.

Seth let loose with a loud yawn.

And he was worried about *her* setting this guy off? Kiva kicked him under the table.

He jerked straight up and seemed more alert.

Kubota kept talking, his voice muffled. "It happened so fast. I tried to get them to stall. My wife was a pilot; she could have stolen a plane if she had to. If only there had been more time. But we launched within the hour." He sat up. "People flooded on. People who were not on the manifest. They took the place of those who were but couldn't get there in time." He shook his head. "I wanted to be with my family, even if it meant staying on Earth. I would rather perish than abandon them and I tried to leave. But security wouldn't let me. I was essential to the project."

"I'm so sorry." Kiva held her breath, expecting him to shout at her.

Instead, he seemed to gather himself. "I had a job to do. Make sure that those of us who did make it on the *Pinatubo* would survive. Once we were in space and everything was running smoothly, I begged to be put in torpor. I didn't want to be aware anymore. And they put me under."

Seth stretched his arms above his head. "For how long?"

"A few years. A few blissful years." He tapped the table. "Then they woke me up. Told me it was my shift."

Seth yawned again, and his eyes drooped.

Kubota glanced his way, but either he didn't notice or care. "With just two of us awake, I had so much time to wander the ship. And think. Too much time to think." His gaze met Kiva's. "Do you know what an impact winter is?"

Although she knew little, Kiva nodded.

"Do you know what happens to the people in one?"

She hadn't considered that in detail.

"My family lived in California where it was warm all year. Oh sure, sometimes we needed a light jacket in the winter, maybe we would turn on the heat now and then. When that meteorite hit . . ." He teared up again. "Temperatures dropped around the globe before we even launched. Within days, crops around the planet would have begun to die. People would have started hoarding, looting. They would know what was going to happen, that supplies would run out, resources. Crime would have peaked." Tears spilled over and he removed his glasses. "Some people, of the doomsday ilk, had stores of food and water. They would have run out eventually, but at least they had a chance. Some hope for a while. A way to feed their children."

His volume elevated and the tempo of his words increased, along with Kiva's heartbeat. She felt he was ramping up his way to something.

Kubota set his glasses on the table and let out a rasping

sob. "My family? We maybe had a pantry full. I didn't plan. I didn't have to! We had passage out." He covered his face for a moment.

Kiva thought perhaps he was done.

But then he dropped his hands. "But my wife and daughter didn't get to use their tickets! Instead—" He gestured wildly in the direction of the torpor chamber. "Instead a bunch of lucky bastards who happened to be in the right place at the right time, they took my wife's place. My daughter's place."

He blew his nose. "And my job was to take care of those usurpers. Monitor their life support, day after day after day. All the time knowing that my wife should be here. My daughter should be here." He took a deep breath. "And, they are not. They're dead. They probably starved to death. Or froze to death. Or—"

Seth's head clomped on the table, his eyes shut.

"Seth?" Kiva touched his shoulder, certain that Kubota wouldn't appreciate one of his uninvited guests dozing in the midst of his tragic story. She shook him. "Seth!"

But Kubota seemed not to care that he'd lost half his audience. "The only reason those people were here, on the ship, was because they took the rightful place of people like my wife and daughter." He pushed the plate of cookies closer to Kiva. "You need more."

She already had two stuffed up her sleeve, but she took

another. There had been close to a dozen to start, there were two left. Kubota had eaten none, which meant that Seth had eaten the rest.

And he was asleep.

Which left her to fill the uncomfortable silence. "What did you do?"

"Henry and I were on a six-month-long shift, caring for the sleeping."

"Henry?" asked Kiva.

"Good man, I thought. But we had a lot of time to talk. Turns out Henry was on vacation in Louisiana with his family. His wife and two daughters. When Holocene hit, they were at a hotel and the owner's son was a contractor at the *Pinatubo* site. Henry and his family got on board." Kubota stopped talking for a moment. "That very day, as he was telling me this? He'd just visited his wife and daughters in the torpor hall."

Kiva said nothing. Kubota was getting more and more riled, and she didn't want to do anything to add to it. Especially with Seth suddenly passed out.

The man put his glasses back on, took a brisk tone. "Henry got me thinking. I went searching for the manifest. The original one naming the True, the ones meant to be on the *Pinatubo*." He curled one hand into a fist and pounded it on the table once. "Because there's no room for the others, the ones with no right to be here."

Kiva's hands trembled. The red monitors on the torpor chambers. Was Henry's family dead? Did Kubota kill them? And Henry? "Is Henry in one of the chambers?"

Kubota clapped a hand over one of hers, startling her. "Oh no. Henry went for a swim one day." His mouth drooped at the corners. "He never made it back."

Kiva froze.

"As for the True." Kubota smiled. "I take good care of them. The True are safe and sound."

She managed to eke out a question. "And the others?"

"They've been taken care of as well." His smile disappeared. "They'll never take the place of anyone again."

Kiva gulped. "But you said they were dead by their own volition."

"Not an untruth by any means. They chose to be usurpers. There was a penalty to pay."

A visual jumped into her head of him meandering the hall of torpor chambers, choosing who would live and who would die, a misguided, vengeful whim. If he truly cared for the future of their civilization, wouldn't all the survivors have equal footing?

Shouldn't they all have a rightful place?

Kiva and her mother would have as much right to survive as Seth and his father.

Kubota's eyes narrowed. "Now tell me, you must be feeling sleepy?"

She said nothing, but her hand felt the hidden hardness up her sleeve.

"Henry turned out to be a fan of my cookies. In the end." He leaned forward. "Everyone says you should wait an hour after eating to swim."

Kiva tried not to react.

The cookies were drugged. She felt stupid for not noticing sooner.

But she hadn't eaten any.

What would Kubota do if he found out?

Kiva yawned, as large as possible without seeming fake. "No, I'm not sleepy." She rubbed her eyes, then opened them wide, as if fighting it.

He watched her.

She set her arm on the table and set her chin in her hand. "Go on." She yawned. "I'm listening." She shut her eyes, trying to slow her breaths even as her heart drummed in her chest with both anger and fear, so hard she was sure he could hear it. Slowly, she let her arm slide down until her head hit the table.

"About time." Kubota's chair squealed as he pushed back.

The cat meowed.

"Oh, Cleo, it had to be done. These two were going to take up far too much of my time. And they were much too curious for their own good." His footsteps went away.

Kiva remained motionless but opened her eyes.

Across the room, he grabbed ahold of the cart and pushed.

Kiva shut her eyes as the screech grew closer and closer. She held her breath when it stopped.

"We'll do the boyfriend first."

He's not my boyfriend.

Kiva was grateful she had thought to face her head away from Seth. She scrunched her eyes shut until the wheels moved again, their screech slowly retreating until it had diminished completely.

She opened her eyes, then sat up and dumped the cookies out of her sleeve.

"Meow." Cleo gazed up at her and blinked.

Seth was gone.

Kiva ran over to the exit, stopping mere inches shy of the doorframe so she could peek into the hallway.

Kubota rounded the corner, pushing the cart in front of him, Seth on top of the crate. He was headed in the direction of the hall with the torpor chambers.

Kiva pressed herself against the wall. Was that his plan? To stick them in torpor with everyone else?

But they could remain there forever, if he didn't decide to throw them in the lake with poor Henry.

Either way, whichever fate, no one would ever know what happened to them.

She had to grab Seth and get out.

But how?

Kiva tiptoed to the end of the hallway and peered around the corner.

Kubota wasn't yet halfway down the corridor to the chamber. That limp hindered his speed. Yet he also seemed in no rush, apparently confident that whatever he'd laced the cookies with would last plenty long enough to seal them in torpor.

The cookies had worked on both Seth and Henry.

What if she had eaten them too?

Kiva shivered.

Beyond him lay the Tomb, their escape.

"Think, Kiva." Even if she was able to haul Seth out of there, the tractor beam would keep them from leaving. She had to turn it off.

The bridge was near where they entered. She could run there, deactivate the subordinate system that controlled the tractor beam, then get Seth.

But she would only have ten minutes once the system shut off before it could be reactivated. She didn't know how far away the Tomb had to be before it was out of range of the tractor beam, but there needed to be as much distance as possible. That whole ten minutes, or as much of it as possible, would give them the best chance of escaping Kubota.

The only way to make it work was to get Seth to their shuttle first, then run back in and shut off the system.

As soon as Kubota entered the torpor room and the door shut, Kiva sprinted past the door and around the first corner. There she crouched, heart pounding. What if he sealed Seth in before going back for her?

She cursed herself for not learning how to unseal the torpor chambers.

But the space was so big, there were so many people.

If Kubota sealed Seth in, she might never find him anyway. She crossed her fingers that Kubota would go back to the dining hall to collect her first.

Otherwise, she would be better off to run for the bridge, turn off the tractor beam, and leave by herself.

"No." Not without Seth.

"I can do this."

She had to.

A few moments later, screeching filled the corridor.

Kiva slid over enough to see.

Kubota began his return to the dining hall with the empty cart. If his glacial pace was the order of the day, Kiva had about five minutes to get Seth back in the shuttle and turn off the tractor beam.

"Not enough," she whispered. There was no way it would work if she waited for him to disappear around the corner.

She slipped off her boots.

When Kubota was only a few yards beyond the entrance to the torpor hall, she stepped into the corridor.

If he turned around, he would catch her.

She ran for the door. As she tried to stop, her stockinged feet slid on the slick floor and went out from under her. She landed hard and rolled, then popped up to sitting.

Kubota's back, and the screeching, continued to recede up the corridor.

Kiva crawled inside the torpor hall. Her breaths were shallow and fast as her heart pounded. Then she clutched her chest. "Thank the Gods."

Seth lay on the floor in front of an open torpor chamber, less than ten feet away.

She stripped off her socks, then ran to him, her feet slapping on the floor. "Seth?" She grabbed his shoulder and shook him.

Nothing. He was out cold.

A few feet away was the wooden crate.

The HCU.

The part they needed to save everyone on the *Krakatoa*.

Her gaze went back to Seth.

No way did she have time to get both back to the Tomb.

She had to choose.

Kiva turned her back to Seth and squeezed one of his feet under each arm to keep his legs tight against her hips.

A groan eked out of her as she lifted. She took a few steps, dragging him as best she could.

His heavy, motionless body was dead weight.

She took only seven hurried steps before she had to stop and rest. "Oh, come on." She barely caught her breath, then lifted, groaned, and pushed forward. Again, she managed about seven steps before she was out of breath.

In the hallway, her efforts were accompanied by the constant sound of the cart's screeching wheels.

Sweat dripped from Kiva's face.

Lift.

Groan.

stepstepstepstepstepstepstep

Drop.

Breathe.

Lift.

Groan.

stepstepstepstepstepstepstep

Drop.

Breathe.

Halfway there, her arm and shoulder and back muscles lit up. With each step, they burned more and more as she continued to inch closer to the shuttle.

At least the discomfort helped distract her from the worry that she was probably not making faster progress than Kubota screeching his way back to the dining hall.

The one bright spot was that her route to the Tomb was far shorter.

She dropped Seth, breathed, and looked up.

The airlock was close. One great push and she would reach it.

"Come on. You can do it."

Lift.

Groan.

stepstepstepstepstepstepstepstepstepstepstepstep

"AUUUGGGGHHHH!"

Stepstepstepstepstep

Drop.

Kiva fell to her knees, panting.

The airlock.

She had done it.

She lifted Seth's legs over the threshold, crawled past, then dragged him inside the Tomb.

She took a moment to catch her breath.

He was safe.

And she was exhausted.

But there was still the business with the tractor beam.

Kiva ran back onto the *Pinatubo* and paused to listen. The screeching was fainter, but still steady.

She headed for the bridge and went directly to the chair that appeared to be the main control panel, hoping the voice command was activated. "Access main controls for subordinate systems."

Nothing.

She scanned the screen for the voice command icon, but didn't find it.

"Okay, you can do this." She pulled up the subordinate systems menu and did a quick search for tractor beam.

"Come on, come on." The subordinate systems appeared to be bundled. She couldn't turn off just one.

The entire cluster would have to be deactivated.

"Well, let's hope I'm not turning off anything very important."

Kiva keyed in the sequence, grateful she had taken time to memorize it.

Words popped up on the screen:

Confirm your command. If deactivated, all subordinate systems will require ten minutes to restart.

Kiva hit the console. "Gods, just do it!"

Subordinate systems will be deactivated in—

The voice command, a male voice not near as calm as Hermione, began to count down.

"Ten, nine, eight . . ."

"Now you decide to speak?"

The loud voice echoed in the hallway as the countdown transmitted all over the ship.

"Seven, six, five . . ."

Kiva bolted from the chair.

In the corridor, she froze.

"Four, three . . ."

The screeching had stopped.

"Two, one. . . ."

An openmouthed Kubota stood at the end of the hallway, staring at her with those bugged-out eyes.

"Subordinate systems deactivating."

Time to run.

14

Kiva took one step and suddenly found herself midair, floundering as she floated upward. "Since when is gravity considered subordinate?" Her hands flattened against the ceiling as she tried to push herself back down, to no avail. The weightless pendant on her necklace obscured a portion of her view as she glanced down the hallway.

Kubota was far more well versed at a gravity-free environment, because he pushed off and gained a few feet in less than a second.

She tried to turn and head for the Tomb, but couldn't reach either side, only able to scrabble along the ceiling hand by hand.

Kubota yelled, "You'd really leave here without your boyfriend?"

"He's not my boyfriend. And—" She stopped before adding that Seth was no longer on the *Pinatubo*. Her eyes widened as she realized how quickly the weightless Kubota gained ground. "I will leave him if I have to."

"You can be together. There's a torpor chamber for you too."

She kept moving, hoping to distract him. "You never meant for us to leave here."

"I take care of the True."

Kiva swallowed.

The man thought that he was smarter than everyone else. And he probably was. But that was also his weakness. He didn't expect anyone to outthink him. Another weakness was his temperament. And he was perfectly content to live an infinite, solitary existence with only a cat for company. Proof in itself he was unstable.

She yelled at him without looking back. "I'm not a True. My mother was never meant to be on the *Krakatoa*."

"I looked up Fai Maxwell. She's on the manifest."

"Seth lied. He thought you might have an issue with my mother not being a True." Kiva glanced back.

Kubota's face reddened. "Not a True?" He pushed off, moving fast.

Kiva's heartbeat sped up, but she kept going.

As he passed the hall of torpor chambers, Kubota called, "You should be in there, with them! You belong with the liars. The usurpers."

"You mean I should be dead." Kiva held her breath.

"Yes! You should be dead!"

Something sharp poked Kiva's leg. "Ow!"

A hissing, claws-out Cleo floated spread-eagled past her.

No time to think, Kiva snatched the cat. Cleo's claws sank into her arm through her sleeve, but Kiva grimaced and held on tight. She pulled the knife out of her waistband and held it to the squirming cat's throat.

"No!" Kubota paused where he was, about ten feet away. "Don't you dare hurt Cleo!"

With both hands full and the cat still clawing any skin within reach, Kiva found her face smashed against the ceiling. "Then let me leave."

Kubota hesitated, as if weighing which mattered more: his pet's deliverance or Kiva's demise?

Kiva hoped she had guessed right.

"You're not taking the HCU."

"I know." *But I am taking Seth.*

"You won't do it."

"Do what?"

"You won't leave your boyfriend." He waved a thumb behind him. "You can't bear the thought of me sealing him away. You'll get me to go in there, maybe you'll put me in a chamber." He smiled. "But it won't work. I'm smarter than you, child. You won't go. You don't have it in you."

Kiva heard a beep from somewhere and remembered that she had less than ten minutes before Kubota could reactivate the tractor beam. Perhaps *far* less, depending on how much time she'd wasted floating around.

He was distracting her, cutting into her escape time.

Was there even enough left to get away?

As if he could read her mind, he laughed. "You'll never leave."

"Watch me." She pried Cleo's claws out of her skin and pinned the struggling cat under one arm. Then she stabbed the knife at the wall and pushed off toward the shuttle.

"Nooo!"

Kiva did not look back. Her heart pounded and sweat ran down her face as she used the knife to gain purchase. With one last heave, she floated through the airlock door where a motionless Seth hovered against the ceiling.

She pushed the cat toward him, then reached down with one foot and kicked the door lock. The door slid shut. Immediately, Kiva hit the floor, along with Seth and a yowling Cleo.

"That hurt." She got to her feet, jumped over Seth's prone body, and sprinted to the bridge. She hit the voice command icon and yelled, "Engage engines! Continue plotted course to *Vesuvius*!"

She held her breath and hoped her wording was good enough for Hermione.

"Engaging engines. Resuming course to Vesuvius.*"*

The shuttle began to move.

Kiva sat down, unsure what to do next. Time was still running out. "Go faster."

"Increasing speed."

The initial thrust of the engine knocked Kiva into the back of the chair.

"Woohoo! I love you, Hermione!"

"Request not understood."

Kiva laughed and threw her fists into the air, then ran out to the glass wall and watched the *Pinatubo* recede. But to be sure, she went back to the bridge to monitor their progress for a little while more. She watched as their flashing green dot quickly left *Pinatubo*'s red dot in the dust. "I did it. I actually did it."

"Request not understood."

Kiva resisted switching off Hermione, who certainly had proven her worth in the last minutes or so. She sat down in the chair. "Notify me if any ship gets within five minutes of tractor beam range."

"Notification alarm set."

"Meow?" Cleo seemed recovered from her bout with weightlessness and rubbed against Kiva's legs.

Despite the fact her arms stung with scratches, Kiva

picked the cat up. "I forgive you. Come on, let's go check on Sleeping Beauty."

Seth was exactly where he'd fallen.

To make sure he was breathing, she set a hand on his chest, which rose and fell at a very slow pace. "You are seriously asleep." She checked his pulse, slow but strong, and decided to get him as far as his cabin. Dragging him there was out of the question; she was too tired. Rolling him would take longer but might not be as hard.

Since she was in no rush, she pushed on Seth's back.

His shirt was wet.

Red stickiness dotted her palm and fingers. "What?" She lifted up his shirt and winced. "Oh no."

Several cuts on his lower back oozed blood; two, possibly three of them, large enough to require stitches. The knife was halfway out of his waistband, blade against his skin. The injuries must have happened as she dragged him. Or when he fell from the ceiling. Maybe a combination of both.

She sighed and set the knife on the floor. "I'm so sorry."

Cleo meowed.

"I can fix him," Kiva said. "Or at least give it a good try." Seth's cabin was closer than hers, and she went straight to the bathroom, hoping for some kind of a medical kit. A hinged metal box, shiny red cross running across the top, sat on in the bottom drawer of the cabinet.

Untouched, neat rows of bandages and gauze made up

the top row. She lifted that off, revealing small brown bottles that rattled when she shook them. Antibiotics might be a good idea; his skin might have been dirty from the lake water.

Finally, Kiva actually knew helpful, tangible things. "Thank you, Fai." But there was no telling how long until he woke up, and until then, he couldn't take a pill. She dug farther and found liquid antibiotics and syringes. "Perfect." At the very bottom lay the things needed to stitch him up.

Quickly, she shoved everything back in the box. The top wouldn't shut, so she cradled the whole thing under one arm, grabbed the pillow and blanket off the bed, and hurried back to Seth.

Kiva dropped to her knees beside him. "Ready." She gently pulled his shirt off over his head and tossed it aside. She dragged him closer to the wall, trying to ignore how strange it felt to be touching his warm, bare chest and back. She propped him up on his right side facing the wall, then stuck the folded pillow in between.

She put on a pair of rubber gloves, then opened up a packet of antiseptic. "If you were awake, I'd tell you this is going to sting." She wiped the worst of the cuts, then opened up more sterile antiseptic packets until all the cuts and abrasions were clean. She took a moment to clean the scratches on her own arms, just to be safe.

Cleo sniffed at the growing pile of debris.

Kiva frowned. "You need to go away." After locking the

cat in her cabin, she stripped off the gloves and snapped on a new pair. Once again, she knelt beside Seth again. "Now . . ."

As she unwrapped the needle and threaded it, she considered the fact that what she was about to do was something she'd done only in virtual reality. Would the ability even translate to the real world?

There was only one way to find out.

"I am so glad you're asleep." Was it better to start with one of the smaller cuts and work her way to the biggest one? "No. You can do this." Besides, there was the possibility he might wake up before it was over. Better to get the worst out of the way while he was definitely still under and feeling no pain.

She bit her bottom lip as her hands hovered above the largest gash. "I've got this. It's no different than a pig."

Seth probably wouldn't appreciate the comparison.

"Stop stalling." After one deep breath, she pierced the skin.

Seth didn't move.

Kiva blew out.

If that didn't wake him up, nothing would. "Okay. Neat and even." She pushed the needle through. His skin seemed more fragile than any she'd worked on. Maybe that would be the only difference between reality and Alexandria.

Either way, one stitch done.

The second matched the first precisely. Her confidence grew as she progressed, to the point that she was almost disappointed that only six stitches were needed to close the wound.

"One down." After tying it off, she moved on to the next.

That cut needed but four stitches, and the last only two.

A quick scrutiny of the other cuts determined they would heal okay without stitches.

She carefully set bandages over all the cuts. "Done."

Seth's back was not pretty, but at least his injuries were clean and would heal well with little danger of infection.

Kiva plucked a syringe out of the box, unwrapped it, and filled it from one of the bottles of antibiotics.

She frowned.

His arm was a good place, but there was a better one.

"I can't believe I'm doing this." She drew Seth's pants down just far enough to reveal a patch of skin on his hip that she wiped with antiseptic. Then, syringe cocked in one hand, she pinched a thick bit of skin in her fingers, inserted the needle, and pushed the plunger.

She yanked his pants back up, then set the syringe down and stripped off the gloves. "I actually did it."

A clump of his hair had fallen forward and hid his eyes.

She pushed it aside and tilted him back a little more so that it wouldn't happen again. As she covered him with the blanket, tucking it up around his chin, her hand brushed his cheek. The skin was rough.

From not shaving?

Her fingertips drifted down to his strong jaw, then further still, until they rested on his muscular shoulder.

A sigh escaped her.

While she had been sheltered in Alexandria, he had been in the real world.

In that time, he had grown up.

For all intents and purposes, she had remained a child.

Before she could stop herself, her lips pressed to his cheek. Her words were but a whisper on his warm skin. "Why did you leave me there?"

No one heard nor answered.

Gently, she set his head on the floor, which looked extremely uncomfortable. He'd been through enough. "That's no good." She sat against the wall next to him and put his head in her lap, his nose nearly poking her in the belly. "Better." She would go get the pillow from her room before he woke.

But first, a moment to rest. Her eyes closed. "Just for a minute."

The minute passed. Then another.

Sleep took over, her breaths soon even and deep.

And the nightmare began.

15

The lake was so warm. Kiva waded *in, face tilted upward to soak in the bright sun. She called "Come on!" and braced herself for the inevitable splash.*

None came.

She turned.

The grass-covered slope was empty.

"Seth?" Goose bumps rose on her arms. "It's not funny."

Bubbles popped on the surface a few feet away.

She smiled. "Two can play at that game."

Kiva inhaled and plunged beneath the surface, arms groping.

Where was he?

Her eyes burned and she shut them.

She grasped something and blinked them open.

Seth's bloated corpse floated inches away from her, his dark, lifeless eyes staring at her as orange fish nibbled bits of flesh off his face.

She screamed.

"Kiva. Kiva!"

Her eyes opened.

She blinked, taking in the white hallway, the lights. Her gaze went down.

Seth looked up at her and gripped her shoulder. "Nightmare?"

She wiped her mouth, hoping she hadn't been drooling. "Yeah."

He set an elbow down to prop himself up, but grimaced. "Ah!" He started to reach for his lower back, but hissed in pain and dropped his head back in her lap.

"Careful!" Kiva set a hand on his top shoulder. "Here. Can you roll onto your stomach?"

"My back hurts."

"I know. Try to stay off it."

He slowly rolled onto his front and laid his head on his arms, the blanket down by his waist.

"Lift up." Kiva slid the pillow under his head. "Better?"

"Thanks." He laid his left cheek on the pillow. "What happened?"

Kiva sat down and rummaged in the medical box, looking for some pills to help with the pain. "Before or after the cookies knocked you out?"

He blinked. "Are you serious?"

"Kubota laced them with something."

He groaned. "How could I be so—"

"Don't feel bad."

"They knocked you out too?"

She shook her head. "I still felt sick. Too sick to eat them. I faked it and hid them in my sleeve."

He gave her a half smile in return. "So why is my back on fire? Was it Kubota? Wait, where is he?" Seth struggled to get up.

"Stop." Kiva set a hand on his upper back, urging him to stay down. "It's okay. He never meant for us to leave."

"The HCU?"

She shook her head. "Probably wasn't even in the crate."

He relaxed and laid his head back on the pillow. "How did we get out?"

"When I realized he had drugged you, I faked being asleep and followed him when he took you to the torpor—"

Seth sucked in a breath. "He was going to seal us in?"

Kiva nodded. "But I dragged you here and then turned off the tractor beam and got us out of range. But I'm so sorry, I forgot about your knife and it must have cut into your back when I dragged you and—"

"Stop." Seth held up a hand. "You did what?"

She swallowed. "I didn't mean to, but I was in a rush and didn't know the knife was there—"

"Keeves." Seth set a hand on her knee. "You dragged me here?"

"I didn't know your back was cut until we got back here or I would've—"

He got to his knees, wincing.

"I'm sorry—"

Seth grabbed both her hands. "Stop saying you're sorry. I don't give a crap about my back. You dragged me here?"

She found herself staring at his bare chest. Her eyes flicked back up.

He tilted his head to the left. "And you turned off the tractor beam and got the Tomb out of there?"

She raised her eyebrows. "Well, when you put it like that, it makes me sound rather . . ."

"Amazing." His dark eyes locked on hers.

Kiva held her breath, unsure what was happening.

She had saved him, saved herself, possibly from an eternity in torpor on the *Pinatubo*. And that *was* amazing.

Seth grimaced and reached for his back. "Gods, it hurts."

Kiva stopped congratulating herself and focused on the pain pills. "There has to be—" She brandished a bottle. "Got it. These will help, let me get you some water."

"Help me up. I'd rather be in my cabin than out here."

She helped him stand, then grabbed his pillow and blanket. He walked gingerly down the hallway.

Kiva entered his cabin first and tossed the pillow at the head of the bed, then spread the blanket out.

Seth crawled onto the bed and lay down.

She got him a glass of water and held out two pills in her palm. "These will help a lot."

Seth took them from her. "Thanks." He put them in his mouth.

"They may knock you out—"

Seth spit them into his hand.

Kiva frowned. "But they'll help with the pain."

"No, no way. I've been out long enough." He glanced up at her. "I'm not leaving you alone again."

"I've managed to take care of myself." *And you* she wanted to add.

He managed a small smile, as if he'd read her thoughts. "I know. But I don't want you to have to save us again. Today was enough."

Part of her was quite relieved he wouldn't be out of it any longer. "But you still should rest. And there are other pills that will help with the pain, just not as much."

"Will they knock me out?"

"No. I'll be right back." She found the pills in the med kit and took her time walking back to his cabin.

His bed was empty.

"Seth?"

He walked out of the bathroom, still shirtless. "Did you do this?" He pointed at his back.

Her shoulders slumped. "I said I was sorry—"

"I mean the bandages."

She swallowed. "Yeah, I did. How did you—"

Seth pointed. "The mirror."

Did he want to know details? "There were so many cuts. Only three of them needed stitches, but one was pretty deep and—"

"Stitches?"

"Some."

"I want to see."

She frowned. "But it's already bandaged."

He reached for his lower back. "I'll take them off myself if I have to."

"Don't!" Kiva went over to him. "Just don't. I'll take one off but you can't touch it, okay?"

He held his palms up. "Okay. I just want to see."

"Come on." Kiva took his arm and pulled him into the bathroom, setting his back to the mirror. "Let me do it." She stared at the bandages.

Which one should she show him?

One of the smaller ones?

"This might sting." Her fingers pried up the edge of the dressing on the biggest cut and peeled it halfway off.

Seth sucked in a breath.

"Okay. Look."

Seth backed up to the mirror and twisted his head around. His eyes narrowed. "How many stitches?"

"That one? Six."

He frowned. "Any others?"

"A few." She shrugged. "The rest just needed cleaning and bandaging."

Seth stared. "I can't believe you did that."

Her shoulders tensed. "It's not like I've done it in the real world before!" What did he expect? She wasn't a doctor. "I've only done it in Alexandria, only on animals." Her heart pounded. "You were the first person I ever stitched up. I did the best—"

"Hey." Seth set a hand on her shoulder.

She couldn't take his condescension. But she also didn't want to have to keep defending herself.

"Keeves."

That nickname again. Was he being patronizing? She had to catch her breath.

He smiled. "I'm impressed. That's all I meant."

She watched him, trying to read his sincerity.

He pulled a folded black shirt out of the cabinet. "I never knew you could do that."

She leaned against the wall. "I didn't know if I could. I mean, if something I did in virtual was also something I could do here."

He pulled the shirt over his head, then lifted an arm. He sucked in a breath.

"Let me help." She held each sleeve out straight so he didn't have to move much to insert his arms, then gently pulled the shirt down in back.

"Thanks," he said.

"You should sit down." She held out the bottle. "And here are the other pills."

He sat down on the edge of the bed. "You sure they won't put me to sleep?"

"Positive."

He took the bottle and twisted the top open. "How many?"

"Two."

Seth asked, "How did you know how to stitch me up?"

"Fai taught me about medicine." She rolled her eyes. "Apparently most of it was modern medicine."

He swallowed the pills. "I never knew that."

"It was after you left." She looked away from him. *After you stopped caring.*

"Sit." He patted the bed beside him. "I want to explain."

Kiva didn't want to know what she did in the past. Whatever she did had made him stop being her friend. Knowing wouldn't change a thing. She took a step back.

He sighed. "Come on."

She sat down as far away from him as she could.

He rubbed his jaw. "What did you think today when you saw the torpor chambers?"

She shot a look at him, then focused on her hands in her lap. "I saw that woman and . . . I couldn't help imagining myself in there. Wondering if that's what I looked like when I was sealed in."

Seth cleared his throat.

Kiva asked, "Did I?"

"You did. Pretty much like that, I mean. The others too." He sounded apologetic.

"How often did you see me? I mean us?"

"At first I saw you every day. I made sure I saw you every day."

Tears welled up in her eyes. "You didn't want to see me in Alexandria when I was awake. Why would you want to see me when I wasn't?"

Seth stared down at the floor. "When they first brought me out of torpor, I was so messed up. My mom was dead, for one, which was hard enough to deal with. Then they told me everything I thought about my life was a lie. And I was surrounded by adults." He swallowed. "I didn't believe them at first. I thought it was all a nightmare. I kept waiting to wake up and be back with my mom and . . . you."

Kiva didn't say anything. "But you didn't come back."

"At first they wouldn't let me. They wanted me to get used to life." He shrugged. "Mostly they worried that I would tell all of you the truth and blow the whole virtual reality program."

"And after that?" She watched him. "When they trusted you not to say anything?"

He stared at the floor. "In the beginning when I went to see you in torpor, it was to convince myself that you, and the others, were still alive. Still here. And I felt sorry for you. You didn't know the truth. You were stuck in there, stuck believing in this world that didn't exist. At first I couldn't wait to go back and see you in Alexandria."

"You keep saying *at first*. What changed?" Her words were sharper than intended. "When did you stop wanting to see us?"

"I grew up." He sighed. "Not being in torpor . . . well. It was hard. I had to learn so much. The adults were always telling me what to do and how to think. And I was alone. I had no one my age to talk to."

"You could have come to Alexandria and talked to me any time you wanted!" Kiva's voice broke.

Seth shook his head. "I couldn't have."

"Why not?" A tear slipped down her cheek and she smeared it away.

He started to reach out a hand, then stopped. "After several months of my new life, awake on the *Krakatoa*, I began to realize that . . . you were the lucky ones."

Kiva huffed. "Are you serious? How were *we* the lucky ones?"

"Gods." He covered his eyes. "You don't get it."

"No, I don't!" Kiva sniffled.

He grabbed her arm and stuck his face in hers. "You had each other! You had a life, you had school. You had sun and rain and wind and fresh air and the river—"

"It wasn't real!"

"But you believed it was. You had no idea what had happened on Earth or that we were actually stuck on a stupid ship where it's dark every day and the same people . . ." His shoulders slumped. "Every time I looked at you . . . you still had everything that I used to have." He released her. "You had everything that I wanted."

Her eyes widened. "You were jealous?"

"Yes. It's why I wouldn't visit school, why I couldn't stand to be with the others." He paused. "Why I didn't want to be with you."

Kiva spoke softly. "That explains why you were so mean whenever I did see you."

"I hated myself for it." He carefully lay down on his side.

"Why didn't you just tell me?" She rubbed her eyes on a sleeve.

"Would it have made a difference?"

She shrugged. "I probably would have left you on the *Pinatubo*."

He grinned.

Kiva said, "I'm not even kidding right now."

"I know." Seth laughed, then held out his hand.

She hesitated before taking hold.

His warm, strong hand enveloped hers as he squeezed. "Thank you, Keeves. For getting me out of there. You didn't have to."

"But I did." She smiled. "Like I wanted to explain *that* to your dad."

"I'm serious. And also . . ." He yanked on her hand a little bit. "I'm sorry."

Kiva didn't know if he was still referring to how he acted in Alexandria. "For what?"

He looked down at their hands, still together. "I was so mad when my dad told me you were coming with me."

She slipped her hand from his. "Why?"

"I knew how you'd react after finding out the truth. Confused. Angry." He shook his head. "I definitely didn't want to be the one to deal with you."

Kiva bristled. He made her sound like she was terrible

to be around. How was she *supposed* to feel after finding out their life was a lie?

Seth said, "I thought it was unfair for him to make me. And I thought . . ."

She waited, knowing he would finish.

And he did. "I thought you wouldn't be of any use."

Her hands clenched at her side.

"Don't get mad." He held out a hand. "I'm trying to tell you that I was wrong. So wrong. I'm sorry about all of it."

"Anything else?" Kiva got up and took a few steps toward the door. "More reasons why you didn't want me to come with? If not, I have other places to be that aren't with you."

Seth winced as he sat straight up. "There's one more reason why I never came to see you in Alexandria."

"Hmmm." Kiva tapped a finger on her lips. "Because you thought I was stupid for not figuring out the truth?"

He gingerly got to his feet. "No, that's not it."

Kiva set her hands on her hips. "Then what? Why did you just leave me there?"

"It's complicated."

"I think I can handle it," she snapped. "You know what? Forget it." She headed for the door.

But in two long strides Seth beat her there and hit the privacy lock on the door.

Her hasty exit was ruined. "You can't do that." She grabbed his arm and tried to push him aside.

He didn't budge. "Can you listen to me for one second?"

With both hands, she pushed on his chest. "Move!"

"Keeves. Please."

The reaction in her gut was hard to ignore, those feelings that bubbled whenever he called her that. Kiva pushed him again. "Let me go."

"Will you stop for one second?"

She glared up at him. "Tell me the one reason why you never came to see me in Alexandria."

"The one *unbelievably* stupid reason is . . ." Seth held her face and pressed his lips firmly to hers.

Kiva couldn't breathe.

Or move.

She could do nothing except feel her heartbeat hammer in her ears.

He moved his lips away from hers and whispered, ". . . because I'm in love with you."

16

"You're what?" Kiva staggered backward and slammed her elbow into the cabinet. "Ow."

Seth reached out a hand. "You okay?"

"Yes." She shook her head. "No! I'm not okay. How can you say something like that?"

He leaned his side against the wall. "Because you wanted to know the truth."

"Let me remind you of the last couple of years." She snapped up one finger. "We saw each other what, like three times?" She snapped up another. "When we did see each other, you made it abundantly clear that it basically pained you to even be in my presence." She paced from the cupboard to the wall and back, then held up a third finger. "You laughed in my face—laughed!—when I asked if you wanted to study with us. I didn't even recognize you as my friend anymore. That Seth was gone."

Seth watched her, but said nothing.

"And when I woke up here on the shuttle? The Tomb, whatever it is." Kiva pointed at him. "You acted like I was the last person you wanted to see." She shook her head. "It wasn't an act. I definitely *was* the last person you wanted to see."

Seth raised his eyebrows. "Finished?"

Kiva sputtered. "I—I—no! I'm not finished."

He crossed his arms. "Then by all means, continue."

But she had nothing more to say. Those were all the things she'd been thinking, all the questions she'd wanted answered.

Which meant that the sole remaining reason she could come up with for him to not want to be around her was that . . .

. . . he hated her.

But if he didn't, then . . .

"But how"—Kiva stared up at those big, brown eyes—"how can you be . . . ?"

"After that?" Seth shrugged. "How can I *not*?"

"But why didn't you let me know?" Kiva took a small step

toward him. "You could have spent more time in Alexandria, you could have told me."

His forehead wrinkled. "It wasn't that simple. You were my best friend. When they unsealed me and I learned the truth, the first thing I wanted was to tell you."

"But they didn't let you."

He shook his head. "And then I went through my own evolution, going from wanting you to be out, to me wanting to be back in. But I knew too much, it wouldn't ever be the same. It was easier to stay in the real world."

She whispered, "I missed you so much."

His shoulders slumped. "It was written all over your face whenever I saw you."

Kiva studied his expression.

Seth seemed sincere. And sad. "I knew it wouldn't do any good to tell you how I felt if I couldn't stay in Alexandria and you couldn't leave."

"You kept it to yourself."

"I did."

She needed to know. "How long have you had feelings for me?"

His eyes shifted from hers to the floor. "Your birthday."

"My birthday?" She tilted her head. "What birthday?"

"Twelfth." He met her eyes for a moment, then glanced back down.

The memory of that day came back. He gave her the bracelet, she kissed him on the cheek. And then, shortly after . . .

"But Seth"—Kiva took another couple of steps toward him—"your mom—"

"I know." His eyes locked on hers. "Everything happened so quickly after that. My grief over her, my confusion over leaving torpor, my anger over it all . . . The worst time of my life."

Kiva leaned her back against the wall. "So for three years you've been keeping this all to yourself?"

"Yes."

Why didn't he ever tell her? "Seth. You could have told me."

He blew out a long breath. "I was afraid."

She swiveled to face him. "Of what?"

Seth pointed at her.

"Of me?" Kiva raised her eyebrows. "Why?"

"What if I was wrong? Maybe all my emotions were just bundled together and I mistakenly got love mixed up in all of them. I was grasping for something and the easiest way out was to convince myself it was love."

She ached for him as he struggled for whatever he was trying to say.

"It was easier to stay away. The longer I went without seeing you, the more the feelings died down. Eventually, I told myself that it had never been anything other than a reaction to the grief and confusion."

She wasn't sure how that made her feel, to hear he was content—even happy—about not seeing her ever again. Even if he was right and she didn't return his feelings, wouldn't having her as a friend be better than nothing? "Why did you visit Alexandria the day of the earthquake?"

"Maybe . . ." He paused. "I wanted to test myself."

That day he had winked at her. For just a moment . . . "You were you that day," she said. "For a couple of seconds, I saw my friend Seth, the one I used to know."

His eyes glistened. "I'm still him."

"Do you even remember that day?"

He avoided her eyes. "I was mean. I had to be."

"No, you didn't."

"Yes, Kiva, I did." Seth's eyes darted to her, then away again. "If I was mean to you, then it meant I didn't have feelings for you. But when you showed up on the shuttle . . ." He hesitated. "You were right before, when you said it wasn't an act. I didn't want you to be here."

She frowned. "But you just said—"

"Listen." He touched her arm. "I had gotten so good at quashing the feelings. I didn't have to see you, so I never had to deal with them. And then you were here. I couldn't leave, there was no avoiding you. And you were upset and you asked too many questions and didn't listen to me and you puked all over . . ."

Kiva cringed.

". . . and I thought the only thing that I felt for you was annoyance, but then . . ." Seth paused. "On the *Pinatubo*, in the Versa Space, you were walking in the wheat field. The sun was shining on your hair and you had the most peaceful expression on your face. You looked so . . ."

She didn't know what he was going to say, but she didn't want to look at him.

"Beautiful."

Her face grew warm.

He spread a hand out on his chest. "Right then, I knew the feelings I had for you were all still there." Seth took her hand. "And they were real."

She stared at his hand. So warm. So strong. "Then how can you be afraid?"

His voice lowered. "After all this, after me finally admitting my true feelings to myself . . ." He lifted her hand to his heart. "What if you don't feel the same?"

Kiva didn't know what to say.

She didn't know how she *felt*.

She had finally stopped hoping that he would come back to Alexandria. No, after that day at the school, she had actually *given up*.

After the earthquake, she believed him dead. She believed she would never see him again.

And when she did see him on the shuttle the first time, it was clear he didn't even want to be friends, let alone anything more than that.

But standing there, so close she heard his breaths, holding his hand . . .

Her stomach fluttered. "I've been mad at you for so long."

He dropped her hand.

Unsure what to do with her hands, she clasped them together. "This whole time, all I wanted from you was answers."

His tone was a little sharp. "Well, you've got them." And there he was, narrowed eyes and clenched jaw, the Seth of the last three years.

Could she believe that the old one was truly still in there?

Were they one and the same?

And if so, could she ever trust him?

Could she ever love him?

Kiva took a deep breath. "Can I be honest? Completely honest?"

Seth stood up straight and rolled his shoulders back. All business, once again.

Kiva tried to ignore the shift. "Part of me is *still* so mad. All that time I spent thinking you weren't my friend. Years, thinking you *hated* me." She shook her head. "The worst part is that you let me believe it."

Seth didn't blink. "Got it." His fist slammed against the privacy lock and the door opened.

He started back for the bed.

"Please, wait." Kiva grasped his hand.

He yanked his hand away. "We're done here." He sat back down on the bed and didn't look her way again.

She managed to hold back the tears until she was in her cabin.

Cleo was curled up on the bed sleeping.

Kiva lay down and cried into the pillow.

He *loved* her?

And oh Gods, that kiss—she forced herself to stop thinking about it—but who *was* he?

She hoped he was still Seth, her friend. Because, even though he was upset, he would eventually understand that she needed time to process, to be alone.

But could she believe in this Seth, the one she seemed to be stuck with?

He was mean, then he was kind. He was curt, then he was patient.

How could she know which Seth he really was?

And until she did . . .

"How can I ever love him back?"

Cleo meowed.

Kiva sniffled and wiped her face with the edge of the blanket.

That was a ridiculous question.

Kiva had feelings for Seth, always had.

Otherwise she would have been happy that he left Alexandria and never came back. She would have rejoiced at his death.

But since she turned twelve years old, she had done nothing but miss him and yearn to see him. She had always wanted his friendship.

And maybe . . . more.

She groaned and hugged the pillow as she stared up at the white ceiling.

But now? What?

After three years of it—and in his defense, yes, he had provided a relatively decent explanation, given what she now knew about coming out of torpor—she was supposed to simply forget?

Maybe his reasoning made her even more confused and angry.

Not to mention hurt.

According to him, after those first few months, he *could* have come back. They would have let him return to school and be her friend. True, he wouldn't have been able to tell her the truth, but he *could have been with her whenever he wanted.*

Wouldn't that have been worth keeping a secret?

It was impossible to ignore the fact that he let his own jealousy and petulance keep them apart. His own choices separated them. Broke up their friendship.

Left her alone.

And Seth was supposed to be the grown-up one.

"He's still a child." Her deep breath turned into a shudder.

Cleo stretched, then rubbed against Kiva's legs.

"I'm done, Cleo. No more crying."

She took a long shower and tried to calm her mind.

She dried off and dressed.

Cleo continued to make a fuss.

"Are you hungry?" Kiva hadn't given any thought to caring for the cat. The decision to take her had been so rash. Was there even any food she could eat?

Her only option was to ask Seth.

As she picked up Cleo, she remembered that Seth didn't know about the cat. *Gods.* "This should go *really* well." Kiva paused at the door to the bridge. "Prepare to get yelled at, Cleo."

Inside, Seth was in his chair, bent over the console.

"There's something I forgot to tell you."

He didn't respond.

Cleo meowed.

Seth whirled around, glowering. "What are we supposed to do with a cat?"

Kiva sat down in her chair. The cat jumped down and started exploring the bridge. "Take care of her."

"Stupid." He glared at the monitor in front of him.

"Well, excuse me. I didn't have much of a choice—"

He snapped, "You could have left it there. There's one choice."

"You mean like when I chose to bring you back here instead of the HCU?"

Seth glared at her. "Regretting that decision already?"

"You don't know!" Kiva kicked the bottom of the console. "You happened to be unconscious at the time. For your information, that cat is the reason we escaped."

"Right," he muttered.

She glanced at him. "She is! After I dragged you back here, I ran to turn off the tractor beam and Kubota trapped me."

Seth sat up straighter. "What did you do?"

"The cat showed up and I remembered my knife, so I grabbed her . . . and threatened to kill her."

Seth's eyebrows rose. "Seriously?"

"Kubota backed off. I was going to throw the cat at him and run, but . . ." She didn't have to take the cat. So why had she? What was the real reason? "He was such an awful man. I knew I could be nice to Cleo and—"

"No." Seth's eyes narrowed slightly. "You took the cat because you miss Sasha."

"That's not true." Kiva frowned. "I . . ."

Seth said nothing.

Kiva slumped into her chair.

He was right.

That was it. She missed Sasha.

She was angry that one of her favorite things in the world had never existed. Her fingertips brushed her empty wrist. Two of her favorite things.

"Whatever, nothing we can do now. There's some really gross fish I would never eat anyway." He tilted his head to the right. "Bowls in that cupboard. Then find the package marked tuna, pour it out, and add water. Should work."

She followed his instructions and took Cleo back to her room to feed her. After the cat was done eating, Kiva realized the cat had nowhere to do her business. She shut her in the bathroom, thinking at least it would be easier to clean any mess in there.

She didn't feel like sitting in her cabin alone. Back on the bridge, she watched Seth's fingers on the screen. "What are you working on?"

"Well, I . . ." He set his hands on his knees.

She frowned. "What?"

"You got me curious about your dad and I started looking."

Kiva leaned far enough over so she could see his screen. "Did you find something?"

"Not really. I've been searching pictures of my parents. And your mom. I figure since your dad was probably on the council, he would show up where they were at least once." He swiped the screen. An image appeared of General Hawk and Sabra.

"I've seen that one." Kiva touched her own monitor. "Here, I'll show you what I found." First to pop up was the one of her mother and Fai, their names below.

Hermione announced, *"S. Stone. F. Maxwell."*

"Do you want the voice command off?" asked Seth.

"It's fine. She saved us earlier, so I rather like her now." Kiva swiped the screen and the image of the handsome man popped up, his name below.

L. T. Kavajecz.

"Ell Tee Ka-vuh-jack."

Kiva froze. "What did she say?"

Seth said, "Repeat, please."

"Ell Tee Ka-vuh-jack."

"Jack!" Kiva grabbed Seth's arm. "Did you hear that? She said Jack."

Seth perused the image. "Did your mom talk about anyone else in the recording?"

"No, just Jack. Do you think this could be him?"

"Possibly." Seth went back to his screen and keyed in Kavajecz.

Instantly, an entry popped up. Seth read it aloud, "Major Laurence Thomas Kavajecz, US Marine Corps. On initial manifest." He scanned.

"He's a True?" said Kiva.

Seth looked at her. "What, are you Kubota now?"

Kiva rolled her eyes. "What else?"

"He took a position on the council and . . . there's another entry here for a year or so after the launch." He squinted.

"What?"

Seth turned to her. "It's about the ship's captain."

"What? What about him?" She wanted to strangle Seth for not getting to it.

"He performed a wedding. Sabra Stone and Major Kavajecz." Seth raised his eyebrows. "I think we just found your dad."

"I don't believe it!" Kiva sprang out of her chair and threw her arms around Seth.

He winced and stiffened.

"Sorry." Awkwardly, she slid back to her own chair, embarrassed at her display. And his reaction. She told herself to forget it. There was no having it both ways. Best to focus on the good news.

Seth cleared his throat and pointed. "There are other entries."

Kiva leaned over the console, eager to find out what she could about her dad. About Jack. "This is so amazing. Thank you."

"I didn't do anything," said Seth. "And it changes nothing."

Kiva wondered if he was talking about the two of them.

But then he added, "It doesn't mean your dad is alive."

She stared at the image. "But I know his name. Maybe, at least, I can find out what happened to him." She smiled. "And you did do something. Thanks."

"Actually, I have something for you." He opened the drawer by his station and pulled out a small wooden box.

She shouldn't have snapped at him earlier. She wanted them to at least be friends, even if it took some time. Maybe he had helped find out about her dad to be nice.

"I've had this so long, I didn't think I'd ever get a chance to give it to you." He opened the box and curled his fist around something, then put the box back in the drawer. He appeared reluctant to give it to her.

She hoped he didn't feel obligated. "Seth, you really don't have to—"

"Truth is, I'm tired of dragging it around."

Her heart sank.

Other than helping her find out about her dad, which probably *was* to satisfy his own curiosity, he had fully returned to being the other Seth.

And it was her fault.

He held out his fist. "Here."

She cupped her palms under his hand. "What is it?"

"It's . . . not really anything." He opened his fist.

Something red dropped into her hands. She gasped. "My bracelet."

"No."

Her eyes rose to his.

"As soon as I was unsealed from torpor, I realized that my birthday gift to you never even existed. And I made you this. Partly to see if I could do something here, in the real world, that I had only done before in virtual reality."

Kiva ran her fingers over the woven strands, the perfectly symmetrical white chevrons. "You obviously could."

He ran a hand over his face. "I thought that I could take it to you in Alexandria."

Kiva stared at the bracelet. "But you couldn't."

"Like I said, it's nothing."

"No, it's not." She wanted to wear it, right there and then. "Put it on me?"

"Don't you have other places to be?"

"Seth, don't." Was he intent on turning every moment sour? She tried to shift it back. "This was nice of you." Her gaze slid to the console. "And you helped find my dad. Can we declare a truce or something?"

He ran a hand through his hair as his eyes roamed the room, seeing everything but her.

She waited.

"Yeah. Truce." Finally, he looked at her. "Here, I got it." He tied the bracelet for her. "Too tight?"

She wiggled her wrist. "Just right." *Déjà vu.* She mused, "Feels like on my birthday."

The skin around his eyes crinkled slightly and he brushed his cheek with his fingers. "Almost."

He remembered.

Kiva wavered.

Seth was still the same Seth; her friend was still there.

He had always been there.

She had been too stubborn, and too angry, to see it.

Could she have brought him back long ago?

The answer to that, if there was one, did not matter.

Only one thing did: what she chose to do next.

"The bracelet is beautiful. Thank you." She leaned forward and kissed his rough, warm cheek.

Seth closed his eyes.

Had he wanted her to do that?

Had he hoped?

She knew a little something about that.

Kiva and hope were old friends.

"Seth?"

His eyes opened, dark brown pools that made it easy to believe she could sink inside if she chose.

If she chose . . .

Kiva set a hand on either side of his face and pressed her lips against his.

Instantly, his hands found her shoulders, slid down to her waist, and pulled her tight, kissing back.

She slipped her arms around his neck.

Like any remaining confusion about her feelings for him, the space between them vanished.

Kiva was in love with him too.

Maybe always had been.

She pulled back slightly, eyes locked but faces not quite touching. "I . . ."

The corners of his mouth turned up. "Are you really going to ruin this by talking right now?" He winked.

Kiva wanted to keep kissing him. She *would*.

But first, he deserved to know her feelings for him.

"Say your piece." Seth kissed her cheek. "I've got all day."

Her Seth was back. She had found him.

Or, possibly, she had helped him find himself. "I want you to know how I feel—"

Hermione interrupted. *"Notification of approaching ship. Within tractor beam range in five minutes, forty seconds. Immediate evasive action encouraged."*

17

Kiva jumped up. "Is it Kubota?" Her heart rate, already elevated from the last few moments, segued easily into outright pounding. "I set the alarm. I didn't want him getting us with the tractor beam again."

"Keeves, sit. I'll see." Seth scanned the monitor.

She dropped into her chair, but couldn't simply sit there. Her voice command was still active. "Please identify the ship."

"Shuttle, S Class. Exact identity unknown."

Seth glanced her way. "One of ours."

"From the *Krakatoa*?" Kiva's mind whirled. "Maybe my dad—"

He set a hand on her knee. "I just meant that S Class signifies a shuttle from one of the four airships."

"They're friendly?"

Seth wrinkled his brow. "Potentially."

Kiva realized his reticence. "Like *Pinatubo* should have been friendly."

"Exactly." He squeezed her knee.

"How do we know without letting them in?"

"Unfortunately, that's the only way to find out." Seth slid open the drawer beside his console and pulled out a knife.

Kiva frowned. "You *are* going to let them in?"

"We'll dock with them. I'll be cautious about it."

Was he about to tell her that he wanted to keep her safe?

She touched his arm. "I'm not going to hide this time."

"Figured that." He held the blade and extended the handle toward her.

She took it.

He pulled out another and slid it up his sleeve.

Kiva asked, "Exactly how many knives did they send with you?"

"Zero. They don't know."

"Won't they miss them?"

"Nope." He twirled his chair to face Kiva, his knees brushing hers. "They're mine. I made them."

She stared at the knife in her hand: the blade, the smooth handle. The craftsmanship was impressive. "You *made* this?"

"It's my hobby. I finagled a small forge out of some hardware on the ship and taught myself." He shrugged. "Couldn't spend all my time making bracelets for girls."

She rolled her eyes.

"Promise me something?" Seth curled a hand around the back of Kiva's neck and pulled her toward him.

She gazed into his eyes. "What?"

"No heroics."

She grabbed a chunk of his hair and tugged. "Only if I have to save your sorry butt again."

"I mean it."

She raised an eyebrow. "You think I don't?"

Seth grinned and held out his hand as he stood up. "Ready?"

Kiva squeezed his hand. "Yes."

Seth said, "Activate docking sequence."

"Docking sequence activated."

Seth held her hand as they hurried down the corridor. Kiva had to nearly jog to keep up with his long strides.

"Docking will commence in three minutes, twenty seconds."

"What if they're armed?" asked Kiva.

Seth stood at the airlock. "We're armed too." He pointed at a screen above their heads. "We'll be able to see them enter the passageway between the two shuttles. If it looks bad, we don't open and we disengage the dock."

She had herself all geared up for a potential confrontation. "Oh."

"You sound disappointed."

Kiva shook her head. "I'm happy to avoid any more conflicts for the day, believe me."

"Docking to commence in one minute. Countdown starting. Sixty, fifty-nine . . ."

Seth kissed her hand before letting go.

As the numbers wound down, Seth put an arm around her shoulders. She leaned into him. Being close to him felt so natural, but still so new. She wasn't sure she would ever get used to the feeling. But at the same time, she never wanted it to stop.

"Keeves, this could actually be amazing. Meeting someone we've never met before."

"Yeah," said Kiva. "We'd never met Kubota before either."

"Still." He dropped his arm and stepped closer to the entrance. "Maybe we'll have a guest for dinner." Before she could naysay, he added, "Someone who isn't out to seal us in torpor for the rest of our lives."

Kiva's small smile was more forced than real because at the same time, her stomach clenched. She didn't want anyone else there.

After three years of hoping and waiting to have her friend back, and then a few marvelous minutes of the more-than-a-friend Seth, she wasn't ready to share. Not yet.

She had already been looking forward to the next week of getting to be there, together, making up for lost time as friends. And carving out new moments as . . . whatever their newfound status was.

"You okay?" he asked.

Kiva gave a quick nod.

She couldn't let Seth know. They were there to complete a mission and she wanted to prove she could be a useful part of that. If they were about to have company, she would be as happy about it as Seth.

Or at least pretend.

". . . seven, six—"

"Best to brace." Seth bent his knees and held his arms out to the side.

Kiva mimicked him.

"—two, one."

The shuttle jolted.

Kiva kept her balance.

All was still.

She straightened back up.

"Now we see." Seth gestured at a small monitor at the side of the door to the passageway.

Kiva stared at the empty passageway on the monitor. A

moment later, movement as a tall, platinum-haired girl about their age, in a long pale blue dress, limped into view.

"She's hurt," said Seth. "Open airlock!"

"Airlock opening."

"Wait!" Before Kiva could protest further, the airlock opened. The girl took two more painful-looking steps, then collapsed into Seth's arms.

"I've got you." He slipped an arm under her legs and scooped her up.

"Are you sure it's safe?" Kiva glanced back down the passageway, partly because she couldn't stand to see that stranger in Seth's arms. "There might be more people."

The girl's voice was weak. "It's just me. I barely escaped."

"From where?" asked Seth.

"The *Pinatubo*."

Seth and Kiva exchanged a look. He asked, "How long ago?"

"A few days ago."

Before they were there.

"The shuttle is not working right. I was terrified it would quit before I reached anywhere . . ." She gasped for a breath.

"It's okay," said Seth. "You're safe now."

"Shouldn't we—" Kiva pointed at the open passage.

"Secure airlock," commanded Seth.

"Securing airlock."

The door shut and Seth carried the girl up the corridor, her long, fine hair fluttering out over his arm.

Kiva followed them to Seth's cabin, where he laid the girl down on his bed. He turned to Kiva. "Can you help her?"

She thought about refusing, then realized she was being a child. *Grow up, Kiva.* This girl was hurt. She set the knife down on the small bedside table. "Once I find out what's wrong, then I'll do my best."

Seth touched her arm. "I'll vouch for your best."

Her whole body warmed. She picked up the medical kit and set it on the end of the bed.

The girl studied her face. "You seem young for a doctor."

Kiva glanced over at Seth.

He jabbed a thumb at his back. "She stitched me up earlier today."

The girl's gaze moved from Seth back to Kiva. She looked afraid. Or in pain. Exhausted, maybe?

More likely all three.

Kiva wasn't sure where to start. Seth's wounds had been obvious, like the open gash in a pig's belly. But this, this was a real patient. The kind that Fai had always tried to prepare her for.

Maybe Kiva needed to think about how she would want to be treated. And if the stranger had a run-in with that madman Kubota? She needed to cut her some slack. Kindly, she asked, "What's your name?"

"Stirling."

"That's Seth. I'm Kiva. Where are you hurt?"

Stirling grimaced and set a hand lightly on her midsection. "It hurts to breathe."

Kiva didn't want to lift her dress up, not with Seth there. Actually, not even if he wasn't. "Did you take a blow?"

Stirling frowned.

"I mean like a hit? Did you run into something that hit you there?"

"Oh. Yes." Stirling didn't elaborate.

Nor did Kiva pry. "Sounds like ribs. There's not much I can do for that. Wrap them maybe. Pain pills."

Stirling nodded. "Pills are fine."

Seth came closer. "Did Kubota do this?"

The girl frowned. "Who?"

"Felix Kubota," repeated Seth. "On the *Pinatubo*."

"Oh yes, yes." Stirling nodded.

But Kiva saw no sign of recognition in her eyes at the mention of Kubota. And a homicidal physicist run amok on an airship was not easy to forget.

Stirling was a liar.

Kiva picked up the bottle of pills that she'd tried to give Seth at first. She shook two out. "These will help with the pain."

Seth took the bottle. "Aren't those the ones that knock you out?"

Stirling's blue eyes grew wide in her pale face. "I don't want to sleep."

"No. These are different." Kiva felt Seth's eyes on her as she got a glass of water and returned.

Stirling took the pills. "Perhaps I will rest a bit now?"

Kiva smiled. "Yes. I'll check back on you in a little bit."

Seth left the room and Kiva followed.

The door shut behind them.

Seth read the label on the bottle. "I could have sworn these were the ones I didn't want to take."

She sighed. "They are."

"You lied to me?"

"I had to. She wouldn't have taken them otherwise."

He got in her face. "Why did you give her those?"

Kiva pointed at the door. "Did you see her reaction to Kubota's name? She has no idea who he is. I don't think she was ever on the *Pinatubo*."

Seth frowned. "But she has the shuttle. She said she escaped from there."

"I don't trust her."

Seth leaned against the wall. "Still, she's obviously hurt. She's not lying about that."

"Maybe." Kiva bit her bottom lip. "You can't see a rib injury. There might be bruising, there might not be."

"Are you saying she faked it?"

Kiva shrugged.

Seth stared down at her. "And you felt the best move was to knock her out?"

"It'll take a little while to work. But yeah. She should be out for a few hours."

Seth slammed a hand against the wall, startling Kiva.

"Oh, come on, Seth, the lies are obvious. Her injury, the *Pinatubo*." She crossed her arms. "I don't trust her."

Seth shook his head. "Say you're right. Say she *is* lying. How are we supposed to find out more now? Like who she really is and where she came from? Or if she is alone."

Valid point. Very much so. "I should have asked you first." Regret seeped into Kiva. Her actions had been a bit hasty. "But I . . . I . . . didn't want her to take over the shuttle."

"Gods, Kiva." Seth scowled. "She's about ninety pounds soaking wet. I think I can handle her if she tries anything. But, you know, thanks for the vote of confidence."

"Seth, that's not why I did it!" She set a hand on his arm.

But he turned away and stomped off toward the bridge.

Kiva leaned back against the wall and slid down to the floor, hands covering her face. "That's not why I did it."

Then why did she?

Because she didn't trust the girl when it came to the safety of the shuttle?

Or because she didn't trust the girl when it came to Seth?

Kiva could not sit there forever. She had to go and fix things.

Seth was mad, she got that.

The better move would have been to consult him, confide her gut feelings. Maybe he would have even agreed with giving Stirling those pills.

But Kiva didn't think before she acted.

And in doing so, she'd taken all control away from Seth and kept it for herself. She was competent; but what she did wasn't right.

Kiva slid up to standing, then trudged to the bridge to apologize.

Seth perched on the front half of his chair, focused on the screen in front of him.

She sat down.

He didn't look at her.

"Seth, I'm sorry."

He didn't respond.

"I didn't think." She sighed. "I thought I knew best."

He grunted and still didn't look at her.

"Fine." She slapped the armrest on her chair. "You want the truth?"

At last, he looked at her.

"No, I don't trust her. But I think there's something else going on. And you are not feeling one hundred percent right now." Did she really want to admit the rest of it? She had no choice. "And maybe part of it was that I was jealous."

He blew out a breath and faced his monitor again. "Nice try."

Kiva frowned. "I'm serious."

"Yeah." He swiped a hand across the screen.

"Seth."

He ignored her.

Kiva stood up and squeezed herself between him and his console, pinning them both in.

He tried to slide out, but there was no room.

"You're going to listen to me."

He stared at her neck.

With a hand at his throat, she raised his chin up. "Look at me."

His eyes roamed the room and finally settled on hers.

"I've been waiting for three years to have you back. As a friend was *fine*, that's all I *knew*, that's all I ever *considered*."

Seth tried to move his chin.

Kiva gripped it harder. "I didn't get to finish before and I'm going to finish now." She shook her head. "I never really thought about anyone as more than a friend. I mean, there was only Rom and Rem and Ada." She rolled her eyes. "And I couldn't see myself liking any of them that way."

Seth tried to hide a smile.

She jerked his chin a little. "When you told me that you

were in love with me . . . it threw me. I didn't know how to react." She sat down on the tabletop and slid her hands to his face. "But I have the same feelings for you that you have for me. And when that shuttle showed up and *she* got out . . ."

The console vibrated beneath her. Kiva ignored it. "I didn't want to share you. Not yet." She leaned forward and kissed him, fully prepared to be rejected.

Instead, he set a hand on her cheek and kissed her back.

She pulled away slightly. "I swear, I never once thought about whether or not you could protect me. It had nothing to do with you."

Seth raised his eyebrows. "Oh, I think it had a little something to do with me."

Once more, the console vibrated.

"Why is my butt buzzing?" She turned around and stared down at the screen. "Is that a ship?"

"What?" Seth held her waist and moved her to the side. "Gods."

The shuttle jolted and came to a stop.

Kiva lost her balance and fell into Seth, knocking him into his chair. He grimaced in pain.

"Sorry!" She jumped back.

The shuttle began to move again.

Seth said, "Tractor beam."

"But how?" Kiva sank into her chair. "I set an alarm!"

"You should have given me pills that worked faster." Stirling staggered onto the bridge.

Kiva and Seth jumped to their feet.

The girl smiled and held up some kind of device. "At least I had enough time to bypass your security. And deactivate your warning." She dropped to her knees.

Neither Kiva nor Seth made a move to help her.

Seth asked, "Whose tractor beam is that?"

But before Stirling could answer, she passed out.

Seth turned back to his console. "It keeps saying unidentified."

"Could it be the *Vesuvius*?" asked Kiva.

"Come on." Seth jogged out the door and down the corridor, Kiva at his heels. At the glass wall, they stared out.

A ship, far bigger than the *Pinatubo*, closed in on them.

Kiva shivered.

Seth took her hand.

"They can't board us with her shuttle blocking the airlock, right?"

"I don't think they're going to board us." Seth pulled her closer. "I think they're bringing the Tomb aboard them."

18

Kiva's heart raced. "I'm scared."

He squeezed her hand. "I won't let anyone hurt you."

"Good to know." She glanced up at him. "But we need a plan."

His gaze dropped to her bare feet. "Get your boots on."

"I left them on the *Pinatubo*." Before he could say anything, she added, "Don't ask."

"Should be more in your cabin. Maybe not boots, but something." He dropped her hand. "Hurry. Meet me back here."

She started to leave. "Wait. What about Cleo?"

"The cat?" Seth looked annoyed, then straightened up. "Bring her."

Kiva frowned. "For real?"

He shrugged. "Gut feeling. Trust mine for once?"

She nodded.

In her cabin, Kiva found a pair of rubber-soled black shoes that turned out to be far more comfortable than the boots. And no laces to tie. Another look around revealed nothing else that she couldn't live without. She grabbed the cat and headed back to meet Seth.

The door to his cabin was open.

She peered in.

Seth's shirt was off and he had his back to the mirror. Two of his bandages were red.

"You're bleeding." Kiva dropped the cat. "Let me see."

Seth shook his head. "There's no time."

"Shut up." Kiva touched his back and carefully pried off the first bandage. The stitches were fine, just some leaking.

Same with the second.

She peeled up the edge of the bandage on the biggest gash and sucked in a breath. Two stitches had ripped out.

Seth asked, "Bad?"

"I should sew it back up."

"That sounds pleasant."

Kiva set a hand on his bare arm. "I'll be gentle."

"Wait," Seth spoke up. "Time until we reach the ship?"

"Eleven minutes until boarding of unknown vessel."

He raised an eyebrow. "You better be gentle *and* fast."

"Lie down." She quickly gathered what she needed and sat on the edge of the bed to tear open the package that held the needle. Her hands trembled, partly from having to stitch Seth while he was awake and partly because she was terrified about what was going to happen when they boarded that ship.

Kiva tried her best to focus on the task at hand. "This is going to hurt."

He pushed his head into the pillow.

She held her breath as she pushed the needle in and through.

Seth didn't move or make a sound through that stitch or the next. He remained silent and motionless for the entire procedure.

As soon as she was done, she applied a new dressing. "Done."

Seth sat up and reached for his shirt, his eyes a little watery.

"Here." Kiva helped him put it on and sat down beside him. "Do you have any idea what we're in for?"

Seth shook his head.

"You should have more antibiotics, just in case." She grabbed the bottle of pills, but stared at the syringe.

Seth eyed both. "Is one better than the other?"

"I think . . ." She held the syringe aloft.

"Do it."

Kiva unwrapped the syringe and stuck the needle in the bottle of meds.

Seth started to roll up a sleeve.

Kiva gestured at his pants.

He raised his eyebrows. "Really?"

She nodded.

Seth stood up and turned his back to her, hands on the waist of his pants. "Wait. When you say *more* antibiotics . . ."

"I've seen it all before." She smiled.

"Well, that's unsettling." Seth pushed his pants down enough to display his bare hip.

Kiva pinched a fold of skin and gave him the shot.

He sucked in a breath. "Done?"

"Yes."

He yanked his pants up. "Okay. We've gotta go." He laced his boots and put the knife back in his sleeve. "You've got yours?"

She glanced at the empty bedside table. "I set it there earlier."

"Get the cat."

Kiva found Cleo in the bathroom and scooped her up, then walked to the bridge.

Seth stooped beside a prone, sleeping Stirling and ran the

flat of his hand down her arms and back. "There we go." He reached down the back of her dress, pulled out the knife, and handed it to Kiva.

They sat down in their chairs.

Kiva asked, "Are we just going to sit here?"

Seth nodded. "They want us, they can come and get us."

She studied his profile.

He seemed calm, confident.

She couldn't stop trembling. "Do you think there's a chance they won't come?"

Seth reached over and took her hand without looking at her. "No. Not much." He sighed. "This was planned. Stirling was a decoy. Got on board and turned off the security." He told Kiva, "I should have listened. You were right."

Kiva slumped down in her chair, still petting the cat. She didn't want to be right. Not this time.

In a deliberate and controlled fashion, the speed of the Tomb decelerated.

"What happens when we reach the ship?" she asked.

"I assume they have a big boarding door that we'll enter. And then they'll detach the other shuttle."

Kiva frowned. "Is the other shuttle still attached to us?"

"For now." Seth scratched his chin. "I wonder how they got it. Or where."

The shuttle stopped.

Kiva's heart pounded.

Seth squeezed her hand. "Let me do the talking."

She was content to stay out of it. "What do you think they want?"

"Outer door has been breached."

"Seth." Her voice trembled.

He leaned closer to her. "I won't let anything happen to you. I promise."

"Says the guy who had to get saved the last time we went on a strange ship." But Kiva's attempt at levity didn't stop the hammering of her heart or her shaking hands. The cat meowed.

"We'll watch out for each other?"

Kiva nodded.

A shout came from down the corridor.

Kiva shut her eyes, but a tear slipped out.

Seth held her hand. "I'm here."

Her eyes opened. Seth's face was blurry. "Don't leave me."

"Never."

A massive bearded man burst onto the bridge, followed by a wiry one with a pale baby face that made him look far younger than he probably was. Both wore thick, red, plaid shirts and faded blue trousers. The bearded giant yelled, "In here!"

The baby-faced man knelt beside Stirling.

Another similarly dressed man entered, wearing tiny tortoiseshell-rimmed glasses. His receding hairline seemed to slip farther back on his head when he smiled at Kiva. "Well, hello there."

Seth dropped her hand and stood up. "We don't want any trouble. You're welcome to food or medical supplies or whatever you need. But then we ask that you leave."

The baby-faced one called out, "Stirling won't wake up."

Kiva said, "We gave her some medicine."

Seth pushed his foot against hers and shook his head.

But it was too late.

"'The lady speaks." The man in glasses came closer. "Where are my manners?" He set a hand on his chest. "I'm Gerard. These are my associates. What's your name?"

Seth stepped between the man and Kiva.

She noticed Seth feeling the cuff of the sleeve that hid his knife. Did he really think he could take on three strangers without getting hurt?

"I'm Kiva." She pushed past Seth.

"Kiva," he whispered.

But she was already moving forward. "Like he said, we don't want any trouble, we—"

But Gerard paid her no attention as he was too busy staring at Cleo. "Is that an actual cat?"

Kiva nodded. "Her name is—"

"Woohoo, boys! You know how happy this will make the witch?" He snatched Cleo from her arms and held the feline aloft.

Kiva reached for her. "No!"

Seth pulled her arm and whispered, "Leave it."

Kiva gulped.

He was right.

If that's all it took to get them to leave, then it was a small price to pay. She said, "Please, be careful with her."

Gerard cradled the cat. "Of course, of course." He stroked the cat. "I had one of these when I was a little boy."

The baby-faced man pointed at Stirling. "Want I should carry her out?"

"Leave her, Pascal," said Gerard. "Not like she's going anywhere."

The giant came closer to Gerard, but kept his distance. He seemed wary of the cat. "Those have a pointy end. I remember that well enough."

"You're such a baby, Josef." Gerard tilted his head at Seth. "Escort this one to the ship."

Seth slipped the knife out of his sleeve.

But Josef was far faster than he looked. With two quick moves, he slapped the knife out of Seth's hand and pinned both his arms behind him.

"Don't hurt him!" cried Kiva.

Gerard stroked the cat and smiled. "That's up to you, my dear. You come with us nicely and your boyfriend here won't get hurt."

"Kiva, no!"

Josef smacked Seth on the head.

"Stop!" Kiva held her palms out. "I'll go. I'll go."

Gerard held out his arm, ushering her to the door. "After you."

Seth lunged and tried to get away, but Josef was too large and too strong. Pascal joined him and they each took one of Seth's arms.

Kiva followed Gerard into the corridor. Gerard said, "They should have the other shuttle disconnected by now."

When they reached the airlock, the other shuttle was gone.

Gerard stepped through and Kiva followed.

She gasped.

The ceiling was close to four stories overhead, the walls at least a hundred yards away on all four sides. Her gaze went down to the battered metal floor, dented in spots. The walls, which apparently had started out white, were dingy and dull.

The only comparison she had was the clean and pristine Tomb, but this ship appeared to have seen far better days. Her eyes scanned the people standing around, all in faded clothes like the others, as weary and worn as their ship.

Stirling's shuttle lay in front of them. Kiva turned around, and other than the letters on the side of the Tomb that spelled *Krakatoa*, the two were identical. The name on the other had worn off; only a faint *a* and *o* remained.

Perhaps that part of Stirling's story had been true, the

shuttle could have been from the *Pinatubo*. Probably stolen, though.

"This way." Gerard led Kiva across the wide space. She snuck a peek behind her.

Josef and Pascal followed, easily restraining a struggling Seth.

Kiva ached to help. She still had her knife. But if she didn't do as they said, she had the feeling they wouldn't hesitate to hurt Seth.

Gerard headed up a flight of stairs, then paused at the top. "She's going to meet us here."

"Who?" asked Kiva.

"The witch."

As if taking the inquiry as her cue to enter, the door opened and an extremely tall and sturdy woman with very short platinum hair stepped out, eyes a deep emerald green. She wore a red plaid shirt and faded blue pants, much like the men.

"I have something for you." Gerard stroked the cat.

If this was the witch Gerard had mentioned, she didn't seem like any Kiva had ever read about or imagined.

A smile played at the edges of the woman's lips. She rubbed the cat's head. "Nice." The word was accented, her regal voice deep and soothing. She turned her attention back to Kiva. "Another gift?"

Kiva's heart pounded as she stared into the woman's eyes. "Why do they call you the witch?"

Gerard stiffened and darted a look at his apparent superior.

The woman raised an eyebrow at him, then gazed down at Kiva. "But surely, my dear, you must know that not all witches are bad." She cleared her throat. "Introductions, please, Gerard. Or has all decorum *completely* abandoned us today?"

"Apologies, Glinda. This is Kiva."

The first name didn't seem enough, so Kiva added the first thing that came to mind, her mom's last name. "Kiva Stone."

Glinda gave Kiva a quick once-over, then tilted her head at Seth. "And the young man?"

"Seth Hawk," said Kiva.

"So formal. And I thought we were on a first name basis." Glinda took the cat from Gerard and her sleeve slid up, revealing a thick gold bracelet dotted by a solitary, sparkling green gem. "Leave us."

"But first." Gerard pointed beyond Seth. "A third gift."

Glinda's eyes narrowed at the Tomb. She shoved the cat back into Gerard's arms and descended the stairs.

Kiva glanced at Gerard.

He waved his hand.

Kiva rushed down the stairs.

Glinda's gaze brushed over Seth, but she seemed far more interested in the Tomb as she ran a hand over the name on the side. "You're from the *Krakatoa*."

Gerard called, "Should I alert Rentz?"

Glinda's green eyes blazed as they raked over all the others standing there. "This is of no concern to Rentz. Everyone clear?"

Heads bowed, and there was some nervous shifting of feet.

Kiva realized every person there was afraid of this woman. Or of what she could do to them. Or have done. Perhaps she was a witch after all.

Glinda asked Seth, "Why are you out here in the middle of nowhere?"

"We need a heat conversion unit for the radioisotope thermoelectric generator."

Kiva took a few steps closer.

"An HCU? That is no minor repair." Glinda snapped her fingers and two men at the back departed through a door on the main level. She asked Seth, "And where are you headed?"

"We thought the *Vesuvius* might have an extra one," said Seth.

"Of course. Another of Trask's four *pets*." Glinda grabbed Kiva just below the bicep.

Seth lunged, but the two men restrained him.

Her grip tightened so much that Kiva's eyes watered. Both corners of Glinda's mouth turned up. "I assume you'd prefer this girl stay alive, yes?"

Seth's eyes stayed locked on Glinda's as if in a trance. "I'll do whatever you want."

Glinda released Kiva.

Kiva rubbed her arm.

"Oh my. If only all my negotiations went this smoothly. I would own the universe by now." Glinda sent a glare around the room, as if not pleased with the silence. All the surrounding people, save Kiva and Seth, joined in the laughter. Apparently satisfied, the woman set her hands on her wide hips. "Let him go, boys." Her eyes narrowed at Seth. "You will behave, I trust?"

Seth nodded.

Josef and Pascal released him.

Seth brushed off his shirt, then straightened his shoulders.

The two men reappeared and set a wooden crate bearing the words SPACE VENTURE at her feet.

"Ah, here's what you need," said Glinda.

Kiva stood up straighter. This ship was obviously not one of Trask's airships, yet it had a Space Venture part. If it was the HCU they needed, did it matter?

Seth's eyebrows knotted together. "And in return?"

"Well, I'll send someone along with you. They can help

install the new HCU, maybe pick up a few things while they're on board."

Kiva watched Seth.

Was he going to agree?

She trusted none of these people, but maybe once they got away, she and Seth could figure out a way to warn the *Krakatoa* they were on their way.

Seth nodded. "Of course."

"Good." Glinda pointed at Pascal. "You go along."

Kiva wasn't thrilled about the company, but if it meant they could leave, she wasn't going to complain.

Glinda smiled at Seth. "You, handsome boy, are free to go."

Seth exhaled, as if he'd been holding his breath. He reached a hand out. "Kiva, come on."

Kiva took a step.

Glinda gripped Kiva's shoulder so hard it hurt. "Was I not clear? It's the HCU. *Or* the girl. This isn't a charity." She waggled a finger at him. "You can't have both."

"No," said Kiva.

Glinda pretended to wave a fan at her head. "Oh, young love. It makes me misty."

Seth locked eyes with Kiva.

Even though she was surrounded by strangers, she relaxed.

Seth would choose her. A shame to leave behind the HCU, but they would soon be on their way to find another.

Seth dropped his outstretched arm and mouthed *I'm sorry.*

Kiva didn't understand.

Then Seth pointed at the crate. "The HCU."

"Load it up!" called Gerard.

The two men carried the crate through the airlock and onto the Tomb.

Kiva took a step toward Seth, expecting to be stopped.

"Go." Glinda waved her on. "Time for farewell."

Kiva ran to Seth. "You can't leave without me."

Seth gripped her shoulders. "Think about everyone on the *Krakatoa*. We need that HCU."

"So now I actually *am* a sacrifice?" Her eyes narrowed and her face burned. "You said you wouldn't leave me. You said *never*."

"You know how important this is."

"Then you stay. I'll take it back to the *Krakatoa*."

Seth's hand tightened on her shoulders. "Please, Keeves—"

"Don't call me that. Don't ever call me that again."

Seth crushed her to him and kissed her.

She slapped him.

Glinda laughed as the crowd around them cooed and catcalled.

Kiva shoved Seth away, then wiped her mouth. "I hate you."

"For now. But I'll be back." He winked. "And then we'll see."

The men came back out from the Tomb, the HCU left on board.

Angry tears blurred Kiva's vision and she swiped at them, refusing to shed even one over him. Seth had given up. He hadn't even fought for her. There had been no negotiations. Glinda had offered and Seth had caved. It had all been so simple—

Kiva sucked in a breath. Too simple. Why would they hand off a perfectly good HCU to strangers?

Gerard called out to a woman behind a console. "Open the bay doors."

"Opening," called the woman.

"And turn off the tractor beam."

The woman called back, "I have to run diagnostics before I can get it back on. The maintenance warning has been on for about a week."

Gerard held up a thumb. "We're not expecting any more company. Go on and shut it down." Then Gerard huddled with Glinda while Pascal and the giant Josef stood between Seth and the Tomb. Glinda passed something to Gerard, and Kiva glimpsed a flash of metal.

A weapon?

Was it meant to be used on Seth? Would they use him to get to the *Krakatoa,* and then when he outlived his usefulness—

Kiva had no way to know for sure, but why wouldn't they

take advantage of the situation? An entire spaceship at their fingertips. Maybe they'd been waiting for such an opportunity to get off their current rust bucket.

There had to be some way to get them both out of there, alive, along with the HCU. Kiva had to at least try. The *Krakatoa*, and all lives on her, depended on them.

The knife dug into her back and she reached for it.

"You'll never get to the *Krakatoa* without him." She held the knife to Seth's neck.

"Whoa." Seth held up his hands. "Keeves, come on."

Gerard and Glinda froze.

Kiva whispered, "I'm trying to get us both out of here."

Glinda took a step forward. "You won't hurt him."

"Try me." Kiva pressed the knife to Seth's skin. He winced as a thin trail of blood dribbled down his neck.

"Fine, fine." Glinda motioned to Josef and Pascal to back off, clearing a path to the Tomb. "There's no need for this."

"I think there is. Move." Kiva nudged Seth.

He inched toward the Tomb as she kept the knife to his throat.

"This is nonsense, you know." Glinda shook her head. "You'll never get out of here."

With only about ten yards left between them and the Tomb, Seth whispered, "We won't both make it." His gaze went to Josef. "Just let me go."

Kiva's grip on the knife tightened. "But if you go with them, they'll kill you once they have the *Krakatoa*."

"How do you know—"

"Gut feeling."

Seth gave her a look as if gauging her confidence. "What's your plan?"

"On three, you run for the airlock."

Josef took a step forward.

"Back off!" said Kiva. "I mean it."

Glinda flicked a hand at him. "Let the girl have her fun."

Seth whispered, "This is wrong. I'm not leaving you."

A corner of Kiva's mouth turned up. "You were fine with it a minute ago."

Their eyes met.

Kiva said, "Get ready."

"I'm not doing this."

"You have to," said Kiva. "*One*."

"What am I supposed to tell your mom?"

"I'm trying to count here."

"Seriously."

"Tell her I saved the *Krakatoa*. *Two*."

Seth said, "I will come back."

"I'm counting on it. *Three!*"

Time slowed.

Seth sprinted for the Tomb.

Kiva leapt forward and plowed into a charging Josef, plunging the blade into his abdomen.

He knocked it aside with one massive paw as he swept Kiva up in the other, dangling her upside down by one foot.

Seth reached the airlock.

Kiva shrieked and struggled to get loose as Josef lunged for the Tomb.

Seth stood in the opening, frozen, staring at Kiva.

"Go!" she screamed.

Seth slammed his hand on the controls, and the door began to close.

Josef swung her body toward the narrowing gap, attempting to block it. Kiva threw out her arms and slammed headfirst into the door just as Seth disappeared from sight, safely inside.

Josef dumped her on the metal deck.

"Oomph." Kiva sat up and rubbed her head. "That's going to leave a mark." She smiled. She'd done it.

"Stop him!" yelled Glinda. "Close the doors!"

Workers scrambled to obey, but there was nothing to be done.

The Tomb was already moving through the inner bay doors. As Kiva watched, the shuttle, along with Seth, disappeared through the bay doors right before they closed with a boom.

Glinda glared at Gerard expectantly.

He shrugged. "You know we can't close the outer bay doors in time."

Glinda swore.

Kiva breathed out. Seth had made it.

"Get him back with the tractor beam!" yelled Glinda.

"We can't," said Gerard. "It's in diagnostic mode."

"Idiots!" Glinda fumed. "Does nothing work around here?"

"Weapons," said Gerard.

Glinda's eyes glinted. "Then blow him out of the stars."

"No!" cried Kiva.

Glinda said, "I told you, this isn't a charity. I don't just hand out spare parts for free." She called over to the woman at the console. "One missile should do it I think."

Pascal came running. "Tell them to stand down."

"And why would I do that?" asked Glinda.

Pascal pointed at the empty bay where the Tomb had been. "Because Stirling is still on board that shuttle."

"Augh!" Glinda's face reddened as she shoved Pascal away. "Why didn't you tell me?"

"I just did," said Pascal meekly.

"Gerard!" yelled Glinda. "Get that shuttle back with my HCU!"

"And Stirling?" he asked.

"Yes. Stupid girl." The woman held a hand to her forehead. "Get her back too." She dropped a hand and stared at Kiva. "And lock her up."

With one arm but no lingering malice, Josef slung Kiva over his shoulder and bore her away to an uncertain future.

Bouncing on his back, she glimpsed once more the empty bay which, moments before, had held both Seth and the Tomb.

A sob caught in her throat.

Even though it had been her idea, she didn't believe that Seth would ever leave without her.

Until he did.

Your world is as you see it to be. Until it isn't.

He had been right.

Less than three days after walking barefoot along the river in Alexandria, Kiva found herself alone, Gods knew where in space, on a squalid ship full of desperate, haggard strangers.

Along with one very angry witch.

ACKNOWLEDGMENTS

A book is never the work of one person, and there are so many others responsible for this one. As always, my editor Liz Szabla tops the list. I am grateful every day for the opportunity to work with her, and this marks our eleventh book together. Macmillan is stocked with so many amazing people, and my thanks go out to Jean Feiwel, Kelsey Marrujo, Anna Poon, and Rich Deas, to name but a few who help get my books out into the world.

My older brother, Steven Stuve, served as technical and science advisor as I aimed to make the science in this book plausible. Any failed efforts in that area are completely the result of my creative mind not grasping his physics dissertation-level emails.

Moral support came from so many places, including regular monthly meetings of my Bagel Bunch crew: Dr. Michael Norman, Shelley Tougas, Michelle Hansen, and Scott Shoemaker.

Huge shout-out to Pamela Klinger Horn, book goddess extraordinaire. Books have never had a truer friend.

Many thanks to my local indie, Chapter 2 Books, for always being a champion of my books.

And of course there are Tim, Bailey, and Tanzie, my reasons for everything.

THANK YOU FOR READING THIS FEIWEL AND FRIENDS BOOK

THE FRIENDS WHO MADE

THE TOMB

POSSIBLE ARE:

JEAN FEIWEL, Publisher

LIZ SZABLA, Associate Publisher

RICH DEAS, Senior Creative Director

HOLLY WEST, Editor

ANNA ROBERTO, Editor

VAL OTAROD, Associate Editor

KAT BRZOZOWSKI, Editor

ALEXEI ESIKOFF, Senior Managing Editor

KIM WAYMER, Senior Production Manager

ANNA POON, Assistant Editor

EMILY SETTLE, Assistant Editor

PATRICK COLLINS, Creative Director